AXE

Ed McBain was born in Manhattan, but fled to the Bronx at the age of twelve. He went through elementary and high school in the New York City school system, and the Navy claimed him in 1944. When he returned two years later, he attended Hunter College. After a variety of jobs, he worked for a literary agent, where he learnt about plotting stories. When his agent-boss started selling them regularly to magazines, and sold a mystery novel and a juvenile science-fiction title as well, they both decided that it would be more profitable for him to stay at home and write full time.

Under his own name, Evan Hunter, he is the author of a number of novels including *The Blackboard Jungle*, *The Paper Dragon* and *Every Little Crook and Nanny*. As Ed McBain he has written the highly popular '87th Precinct' series of crime novels including *Shotgun*, *He Who Hesitates*, *Fuzz*, *Hail, Hail, the Gang's All Here!* and *Sadie When She Died*

Ed McBain

AXE
An 87th Precinct Mystery

SEVERN
SH
HOUSE

This edition published in Great Britain 1990 by
SEVERN HOUSE PUBLISHERS LTD of
35 Manor Road, Wallington, Surrey SM6 0BW
First published in Great Britain 1964 by Hamish Hamilton Ltd

British Library Cataloguing in Publication Data
McBain, Ed, *1926—*
  Axe.
  I. Title
  818'.54 [F]

ISBN 0-7278-1722-1

Printed and bound in Great Britain
at the University Press, Cambridge

This is for
Barbara and Leonard Harris

The city in these pages is imaginary.
The people, the places, are all fictitious.
Only the police routine is based on
established investigatory technique.

one

January.

It refuses to obey the clichés this year. December did not provide a white Christmas, and now there is no lingering snow on the city pavements. The clouds above the jagged skyline are threatening, but it is too warm to snow, and yet there is no real warmth. Neither is there a blustering wind, or frost-rimmed windows. There is instead a sunless lack of cheer, an overall impression of solemn monochromatic grey.

The grey descends from the curving sky in motion, covers the motionless city buildings, grey themselves with the soot of centuries, extends to the grey concrete pavements and the deeper grey of asphalt streets, becomes a part of the residents themselves, a teeming grey mass that moves along the city streets as though suspended in melancholy, captured in the doldrums of January. This is the first month. It contains thirty-one days, year in and year out. There will be no future days or years for the man lying against the basement wall.

An axe is embedded in his skull.

It is not a hatchet, it is an axe; designed for the felling of trees and the chopping of wood. Its wedge-shaped metallic striking head has been driven with astonishing force into the man's skull, splitting it wide, covering blade and hair and face and floor and wall with blood and brain matter. There is no question but that this was the final blow, and the condition of the dead man makes it equally clear that this final blow was not at all necessary: there are more than twenty other wounds on the man's face and body. His jugular is severed and pouring blood, his fingers and hands are mutilated from the repeated slashing of the axe head as he raised his hands to ward off the savage blows. His left arm dangles loosely from the shoulder where a vicious cleaving blow of the axe has left a wide trench across skin and bone. He was undoubtedly dead even before his assassin drove the axe blade into his skull and left it there, the curving wooden handle arcing against the grey wall, the wood stained with blood and pulp.

Blood has no aroma.

There was the smell of coal dust in the basement, and the smell of human sweat, and even the smell of urine from behind one of the coal bins near the furnace, but Detective Steve Carella could smell no blood. The police photographers were snapping pictures and the assistant medical examiner was pronouncing the man dead and waiting for the lab boys to chalk his position on the floor before carting him off to the morgue for autopsy, as if autopsy were needed with an axe sticking out of his head. Detective Cotton Hawes was talking to the two cops sent over by Homicide, and Carella was bent on his knees before a boy of about seven years old who kept trying desperately not to look at the bloody corpse against the wall.

'All right, sonny, what's your name?' Carella said.

'Mickey,' the boy answered.

'Mickey what?'

'Mickey Ryan. Will there be a ghost?'

'No, son, no ghost.'

'How can you tell?'

'There's no such things as ghosts,' Carella said.

'That's what you think,' Mickey said. 'My father saw a ghost one time.'

'Well, there won't be a ghost this time,' Carella said. 'You want to tell me what happened, Mickey?'

'I came down to get my bike, and I found him,' Mickey said. 'That's all.'

'Right where he is? Against the wall there?'

Mickey nodded.

'Where's your bike, Mickey?'

'Over there. Behind the bin.'

'Well, what brought you over here, on this side of the bin? Did you hear something?'

'No.'

'Then what brought you here? Your bike is all the way over on the other side there.'

'The blood,' Mickey said.

8

'What?'

'The blood was running across the floor, and I looked down and saw it, and I wondered what it was, so I went to take a look. That's when I saw Mr Lasser.'

'Is that his name?'

'Yes. Mr Lasser.'

'Would you know his first name?'

'George.'

'George Lasser, is that right?'

Mickey nodded.

'And Mr Lasser is superintendent of the building, is that right?'

'Yeah,' Mickey said, and he nodded again.

'All right, Mickey. After you saw Mr Lasser, what did you do?'

'I ran.'

'Where?'

'Upstairs.'

'Upstairs where?'

'To my mother.'

'And then what?'

'I told her Mr Lasser was dead in the basement with an axe in his head.'

'And then what?'

'Then she said, "Are you sure?" and I said I was sure, so she called the police.'

'Mickey, did you see anyone in the basement besides Mr Lasser?'

'No.'

'Did you see anyone while you were going *down* to the basement?'

'No.'

'While you were running upstairs?'

'No.'

'Excuse me, but would you mind?' a voice said, and Carella looked up to where a very tall, plain blonde woman wearing a light topcoat had pushed her way past a patrolman near the basement door.

'I'm the boy's mother,' she said. 'I don't know what the legality of this is, but I'm sure you're not permitted to question a

9

seven-year-old boy in the basement of a building! Or anywhere, for that matter.'

'Mrs Ryan, I understand my partner asked your permission before we . . .'

'He didn't tell me you were going to take the boy down here again.'

'I'm sure he . . .'

'I turn my back for *one* minute, and the next thing I know both your partner and the boy are gone, and I haven't the *faint*est clue where. I mean, I'm pretty upset, *any*way, as you can imagine, my seven-year-old son finding a *body* in the basement with an *axe* in the head no less, so here he *van*ishes from the apartment, and I don't know where he's gone.'

'He's been here all along, Mrs Ryan,' Carella said. 'Safe and sound.'

'Yes, with a corpse all full of blood staring him in the face not ten feet away from him.'

'I'm sorry, Mrs Ryan.'

'My point is he's only seven years old and he shouldn't be put through this sort of ordeal. We don't live in Russia, you know.'

'No, ma'am. But he *did* discover the body, and we thought it might be easier for him to réconstruct what happened if we . . .'

'Well, if you don't mind, I think he's reconstructed enough,' Mrs Ryan said.

'Of course, Mrs Ryan,' Carella said. 'Thank you for your co-operation.'

'Is that meant to be sarcastic?' Mrs Ryan asked.

'No, ma'am, I meant it sincerely,' Carella said.

'Yeah, cops,' Mrs Ryan said, and she took her son's hand and pulled him out of the basement.

Carella sighed and walked over to where Hawes was talking with the two Homicide cops. He did not recognize either of the two men.

'My name's Carella,' he said, 'the eight-seven.'

'I'm Phelps,' one of the Homicide cops said.

'I'm Forbes,' the other said.

'Where's Monoghan and Monroe?' Carella asked.

'Vacation,' Phelps said.

'In January?'

'Why not?' Forbes said.

'They both got nice places down in Miami,' Phelps said.

'No reason they shouldn't go there in January,' Forbes said.

'Best time of the year for Florida,' Phelps said.

'Certainly,' Forbes said.

'What've you got so far?' Phelps asked, changing the subject.

'Man's name is George Lasser,' Carella said. 'He was super-intendent of the building.'

'That's what I got from the tenants,' Hawes said.

'Any idea how old he was, Cotton?'

'The tenants put him in his late eighties.'

'Why'd anyone want to kill a man that old?' Forbes asked.

'Ready to kick off anyway,' Phelps said.

'We had a killing once over near Seventh and Culver,' Forbes said, 'you know the area?'

'Mmm,' Carella said.

'Guy was a hundred and two years old. In fact, it was his birthday.'

'No kidding?'

'No kidding. Somebody shot him while he was cutting his birthday cake. Fell right into the damn thing, a hundred and three candles on it, one to grow on, you know. Guy dropped dead instantly.'

'Who did it?' Hawes asked.

'His mother,' Forbes said.

There was a short silence, and then Hawes said, 'I thought you said the guy was a hundred and two years old.'

'That's right,' Forbes said.

'Then how old was his mother?'

'A hundred and eighteen. She got married when she was sixteen.'

'Why'd she kill him?'

'She couldn't get along with his wife.'

'I see. He had a wife, too, huh?'

'Sure.'

'How old was *she*?'

'Twenty-seven.'

'Oh, come on,' Hawes said.

'He thinks I'm kidding,' Forbes said, pushing his elbow into Phelps' ribs.

11

'No, he ain't kidding,' Phelps said, laughing.

'Over in Homicide,' Forbes said, 'we get all kinds.'

'I'll bet you do,' Hawes said.

Phelps looked at his watch. 'Well, time we was running along,' he said. 'You boys keep us informed now, huh?'

'In triplicate, huh?' Forbes said.

'We're surprised you come out at all on such a cold day,' Carella said.

'It ain't so cold,' Forbes said. 'Over in Homicide, boy, we get days you could freeze.'

'Listen,' Hawes said, as though suddenly inspired, 'why don't you fellows handle this case yourself?'

'Nope,' Forbes said.

'Not allowed to,' Phelps said.

'Against regulations,' Forbes said.

'Homicide is to be investigated by the precinct handling the initial complaint,' Phelps said.

'Sure, but I thought . . .'

'Nope.'

'I thought,' Hawes said, 'that since you've had experience with geriatric cases, perhaps you'd . . .'

'*What* kind of cases?'

'Geriatric,' Hawes said.

'Jerry *who*?'

'Well, I just thought it was an idea,' Hawes said.

From the corner of his eye, Carella saw the patrolman at the basement steps signalling to him.

'Excuse me,' he said, and walked rapidly to the steps. 'What is it?' he asked the patrolman.

'Steve, we got a guy outside, found wandering around in the alley without a jacket on or anything. I mean, this ain't weather to go running around in your shirtsleeves, you know what I mean? It's forty-two degrees out there.'

'Where is he?' Carella said.

'We got him upstairs.'

Carella turned and gestured to Hawes. Hawes moved away from the Homicide cops.

'What is it?'

'Patrolmen found a wanderer in the alley. In his shirt-sleeves.'

'Uh-oh,' Hawes said.

12

The man they had found wandering in the alley was a huge Negro wearing only dungaree trousers and a white shirt open at the throat. He was very black, and very mean-looking, with a scar across the bridge of his nose and with enormous muscles bulging beneath the white cotton of his shirt. He was wearing sneakers, and he seemed to be balancing himself on the balls of his feet as Carella and Hawes approached, almost as though ready to begin throwing punches. A patrolman was standing alongside him with his nightstick in his hands, but the Negro paid no attention at all to him. With his eyes slitted, his legs wide-spread, and his weight balanced, he watched the approaching detectives.

'What's your name?' Carella said.

'Sam.'

'Sam what?'

'Sam Whitson.'

'What were you doing in the alley out there, Sam?'

'I works here in this building,' Whitson said.

'What do you mean?'

'I works for Mr Lasser,' Whitson said.

'Doing what?'

'I chops wood for him,' Whitson said.

There was a deep silence for the space of a heartbeat. Carella glanced at Hawes and then back to Whitson. The two patrolmen – the one who had been standing alongside Whitson with his nightstick at the ready, and the one who had come to fetch Carella – both stepped a pace backward from the huge Negro, their hands moving imperceptibly towards their service revolvers.

'What were you doing in the alley, Sam?' Carella asked.

'I tole you,' Whitson said. 'I works for Mr Lasser. I chops wood for him.'

'You were chopping wood out there?'

'Yes, sir,' Whitson said, then shook his head violently. 'No, sir. I was gettin' *ready* to chop my wood, yes, sir.'

'How were you doing that?' Hawes asked. 'Getting ready, I mean.'

'Well, I was on my way to get the axe.'

'Where was the axe?'

'We keep it in the tool shed.'

'Where's that?'

13

'Out back.'

'Out back where?'

'In the tool shed,' Whitson said.

'You trying to get smart with me, Whitson?' Hawes asked.

'No, sir.'

'Well, take my advice, don't.'

'I wasn't,' Whitson said.

Carella, watching, said nothing. There was a mean and menacing look on the Negro's face, and his size was frightening. He looked as if he were capable of tearing the building down with his bare hands, and it did indeed seem as if he were answering Hawes' questions in a deliberately evasive and somewhat snotty manner, perhaps in order to provoke a fight. Carella had no doubt that if this man decided to begin swinging, he would not stop swinging until everyone and everything in sight had been reduced to rubble. Confronted with a man as strong and as big as this one, the best thing anyone could do would be to tip his hat, say 'Good afternoon,' and get the hell home. Unless you happened to be a cop, in which case you wondered why Whitson had been roaming around in an alley in his shirtsleeves with the temperature at forty-two degrees and a dead man with an axe in his head here in the basement. You wondered about such things, and you let Whitson know that you expected straight answers to straight questions without any crap, while all the time you figured he might just possibly reach out and pick you up in one hand and squeeze you to a pulp in his fist; listen, who told you to become a cop?

'You want to tell me where that tool shed is?' Hawes said.

'I already tole you. Out back.'

'How about pinpointing it for me, Whitson?'

'What do you mean?'

'Tell me where it is exactly.'

'Near the clothesline.'

'Where's that?'

'Near the pole.'

'And where's that?'

'Out back,' Whitson said.

'Okay, wise guy,' Hawes said. 'If that's the way you . . .'

'No hold it a second, Cotton,' Carella said. Listening to Whitson, he had suddenly realized that the man was really trying his best to co-operate. But he happened to look surly and evil, and his size was terrifying, and he wasn't really very bright. So he stood there like a huge blinking monster ready to wreak seven kinds of havoc, answering questions as well as he could, and coming across only as a wise guy spoiling for a fight.

'Sam,' Carella said gently, 'Mr Lasser is dead.'

Whitson blinked. 'What you mean?' he asked.

'He's dead. Someone killed him. Now, Sam, you'd better pay close attention to what we ask you, and you'd better tell the truth when you answer, because now that you know someone's been killed, you also know you can get in a lot of trouble. Okay?'

'I didn't kill him,' Whitson said.

'No one said you did. We just want to know what you were doing out in the alley in only your shirt in this kind of weather.'

'My job is chopping the wood,' Whitson said.

'What wood?'

'The firewood.'

'Sam, the furnace in this building burns coal.'

'Yes, sir.'

'Then why do you chop firewood?'

'Some of the tenants, they got fireplaces in they apartments. Mr Lasser brings logs to work with him in his truck, and I splits them up for him, and he gives me fifty cents an hour. Then he sells the firewood to the tenants.'

'Do you work for him every day, Sam?'

'No, sir. I come to work every Wednesday and Friday. But this year, Wednesday is New Year's Day, and Mr Lasser he say I shouldn't come in, so I didn't come in Wednesday this week. I come in today instead. Friday.'

'Do you always come in at this time?'

'Yes, sir. Three o'clock in the afternoon. Yes, sir, that's the time I usually comes in.'

'Why so late?'

'Well, I got jobs in other buildings around.'

'Doing what?'

'Helping out the supers.'

'How'd you happen to get this job with Mr Lasser?' Carella asked.

'I got it for him,' a voice just outside the open foyer door said, and they all turned to find themselves looking at a thin Negro

15

woman with a scowl on her face and fire in her eyes. She was wearing a flowered house dress and a pair of men's house slippers, but she walked past the patrolman with great dignity, and took up a position beside Whitson, her back ramrod stiff, her head high. Standing beside the huge Whitson, she seemed even more thin and fragile than she really was. But Carella, watching her, suddenly noticed the similarity of her features and Whitson's, and realized the woman was Whitson's mother. As if to corroborate his guess, she immediately said, 'What have you been doing to my boy?'

'Are you his mother, ma'am?' Hawes asked.

'I am,' she said. She had a clipped manner of speaking, and she held her head cocked to one side as though drawing a bead on the speaker and ready to let him have it right between the eyes if he said anything contrary to her way of thinking. She kept her lips pursed as she watched, her arms folded across her narrow breast, her body balanced exactly the way her son had balanced his earlier, as though expecting a lynch party at the front door almost anytime now.

'We were asking him some questions,' Carella said.

'My son didn't kill Mr Lasser,' she said, looking Carella directly in the eye.

'No one said he did, Mrs Whitson,' Carella answered, looking her back in the eye.

'Then what are you questioning him about?'

'Mrs Whitson, about a half-hour ago, at exactly two twenty-seven to be exact, actually more than a half-hour ago, we received a telephone call from a Mrs Ryan in this building who told us her son had seen the building superintendent dead in the basement with an axe sticking out of his skull. We got over here as soon as we could, and located the body down there near one of the coal bins, and then talked to some of the tenants and the boy who'd found the body, and that was when one of our patrolmen found your son wandering around outside in his shirtsleeves.'

'What of it?' Mrs Whitson snapped.

'Pretty cold to be walking around in his shirt-sleeves,' Carella said.

'Cold for who?'

'For anyone.'

'For someone chopping wood?' Mrs Whitson asked.

'He wasn't chopping wood, ma'am.'

'He was about to,' Mrs Whitson said.

'How do you know that?'

'He gets paid for chopping wood, and that's why he comes here,' Mrs Whitson said.

'Do you work in this building, too?' Carella asked.

'Yes. I do the floors and windows.'

'And you got this job for your son?'

'Yes. I knew Mr Lasser needed someone to split those big logs he brings in from the country, and I suggested my son. He's a good worker.'

'Do you always work outside in your shirtsleeves, Sam?' Carella asked.

'He always does,' Mrs Whitson answered.

'I asked him,' Carella said.

'Tell him, son.'

'I always does,' Whitson said.

'Were you wearing a coat when you came to work today?' Hawes asked.

'No, sir. I was wearing my Eisenhower jacket.'

'You were in the Army?'

'He fought in the Korean war,' Mrs Whitson said. 'He was wounded twice, and he lost all the toes on his left foot from frostbite.'

'Yes, sir, I was in the Army,' Whitson said softly.

'Where's your jacket now?'

'I put it on the garbage cans out back.'

'When did you do that?'

'When I headed for the tool shed. You see, Mr Lasser dumps the logs right out back there in the alley near the shed, and that's where I chops them up. So what I usually does, I come right down the alley and I puts my jacket on the garbage cans, and then I goes to the shed to get the axe and begin work. Only today, I couldn't begin work because this policeman, he stop me.'

'Then you don't know whether or not the axe is still in that shed, do you?'

'No, sir.'

'How many axes are in that shed, usually?'

'Just the one, sir.'

Carella turned to the nearest patrolman. 'Murray, you want

17

to check out back? See if there's a jacket on those garbage cans, like he says, and also look in the shed for an axe.'

'You're not gonna find no axe out there,' Mrs Whitson said.

'How do you know?'

'Because it's right down there in the basement, ain't it? Sticking in Mr Lasser's head?'

two

They did not, as Mrs Whitson had prophesied, find an axe in the tool shed out back, the only axe anywhere in the vicinity being the one that had thoughtlessly been left protruding from the dead Mr Lasser's cranium. They did, however, find Whitson's Eisenhower jacket draped over one of the garbage cans where he had allegedly left it before heading for the tool shed. And they did find a dozen or so rather large logs dumped in the alleyway several feet from the tool shed, all of which seemed to corroborate Whitson's story. They advised Whitson to go home but not to leave the city as they might want to contact him again at a later time, the later time they had in mind being the time the police laboratory reported on the axe handle attached to the axe blade attached to Mr Lasser's head. They were hopeful, you see, that the lab would find some fingerprints on the weapon, thereby enabling them to solve the case almost before the crime was several hours old.

Some days, though, you can't make a nickel.

The lab found an awful lot of smeared blood on the wooden axe handle, and a few grey hairs caught on some of the wood splinters, and also some pulp that had spattered out of Lasser's open skull when the metal blade wedged its way into bone and brain, but alas they found no fingerprints. Moreover, although there were some bloody palmprints and thumbprints on the grey basement wall, the laboratory technicians discovered that these prints had been left by Mr Lasser himself, either as he backed away from his assailant or else as he groped the wall for support

18

when collapsing to the floor after, most likely, the blow that had severed his jugular. It was the medical examiner's opinion that Mr Lasser had been lying on the basement floor already dead for several minutes when the axe was finally sunk and left in his skull, a conjecture that seemed corroborated by the severed jugular and the unusually large amount of blood all over the basement floor, the trickle of which had first attracted young Mickey Ryan to the body. Utilizing a simple logical progression, and beginning with the inescapable position of the axe, embedded as it was in the skull of Mr Lasser, it necessarily followed that this was the ultimate blow and that it had been preceded by numerous other blows. Neither the lab nor the medical examiner's office could suggest when the jugular had been severed, but they agreed on the number of axe slashes -- they each counted twenty-seven, including the dangling fingers on the left hand – and assured the slashing of the jugular had been the cause of death, the previous slashes being serious enough to have caused considerable loss of blood over an extended period of time, but none of them being serious enough in themselves to have caused immediate death. It was the blow across the throat then, a blow that must have been delivered with a sweeping sidearm motion, like the swinging of a baseball bat, that had killed George Lasser. The final axe stroke was something of a *coup de grâce*, the downward swing of the blade into the skull of the man already dead at the assassin's feet and then, the final touch, the leaving of the axe in his skull as though the skull were the stump of a tree and the sinking of metal into pulp signalled the end of the working day.

To tell the truth, it was all pretty goddamn gory.

They had learned from the tenants in the building that Mr Lasser lived somewhere in New Essex, some fifteen minutes outside of the city, a fact which was substantiated by a driver's licence found in the old man's right hip trouser pocket. The licence gave his full name as George Nelson Lasser, his address as 1529 Westerfield in New Essex, his sex as male, his weight as one hundred and sixty one pounds, his height as five feet ten inches, and his date of birth as October 15, 1877, which made him eighty-seven years old at the time of his death.

There was a bleakness to the January countryside as the

detectives drove out of the city and headed for New Essex. The heater in Hawes' 1961 Oldsmobile convertible was on the blink, and the windows kept fogging with their exhaled breaths, and then freezing over with a thin film of ice which they scraped at with gloved hands. The trees lining the road were bare, the landscape sere and withered; it almost seemed as though death had extended itself from that city basement into the surrounding countryside, stilling the land with its hoary breath.

1529 Westerfield was an English Tudor reproduction set some forty feet back from the sidewalk on a New Essex street lined with similar reproductions. Smoke boiled up out of chimney pots, adding a deeper grey to the sky's monotone. There was a feeling of contained and cloistered warmth on that street, a suburban block locked in potbellied privacy against the wintry day outside, defying intrusion. They parked the convertible at the kerb in front of the house and walked up the slate path to the front door. An old wrought-iron bell pull was to the right of the door. Hawes pulled it, and the detectives waited for someone to answer.

There was lunacy in the old woman's eyes.

She pulled open the door with a suddenness that was startling, and the first thing each man saw about her was her eyes, and the first thought that occurred to each of them separately was that they were looking at a woman who was mad.

'Yes?' the woman asked.

She was an old woman, perhaps seventy-five, perhaps eighty. Carella found it difficult to pinpoint a person's age once the borderline of real vintage had been crossed. Her hair was white, and her face was wrinkled but full and fleshy, with lopsided eyebrows that added a further dimension of madness to the certainly mad eyes. The eyes themselves were blue. They watched the detectives unblinkingly. There was dark suspicion in those pale blue eyes, and there was secret mirth, a mirth that echoed humourless laughter in endlessly long and hollow corridors. There was a sly appraisal peering out of the skull, and there was as well a flirtatiousness that seemed ludicrous in a woman so old, a coquettishness that was almost obscene. The eyes combined all these things in a medley of contradiction that was at once blatant and frightening. The woman was mad, her eyes shouted the fact to the world. The woman was mad, and her madness sent a shudder up the spine.

'Is this the home of George Nelson Lasser?' Carella asked, watching the woman, wanting nothing more than to be back at the precinct where there was order and dimension and sanity.

'This is his home,' the woman replied. 'Who are you and what do you want?'

'We're detectives,' Carella said. He showed her his shield and his identification card. He paused a moment, and then said, 'May I ask who I'm talking to, ma'am?'

'Whom, and you may not,' she said.

'What?'

'Whom,' she said.

'Ma'am, I . . .'

'Your grammar is bad, and your granpa is worse,' the woman said, and began laughing.

'Who is it?' a voice behind her said, and Carella glanced up to see a tall man stepping from the comparative darkness beyond the entrance door into the gloomy arc of light proscribed by the door's opening. The man was in his early forties, tall and thin, with light brown hair that hung haphazardly on his forehead. His eyes were as blue as the madwoman's, and Carella knew at once that they were mother and son, and then reflected briefly upon the mother–son combinations he had met this day, starting with Mickey Ryan who had found a dead man in a basement, and moving through Sam Whitson who chopped wood with an axe, and now onto this tall, poised man with an angry scowl on his face who stood behind and slightly to the right of his demented mother while demanding to know who these men were at the front door.

'Police,' Carella said, and again he flashed the tin and the card.

'What do you want?'

'Who are you, sir?' Carella asked.

'My name is Anthony Lasser. What do you want?'

'Mr Lasser,' Carella said, 'is George Lasser your father?'

'He is.'

'I'm sorry to have to tell you he is dead,' Carella said, and the words sounded stiff and barely sympathetic, and he regretted having had to report them, but there they were, hanging on the air in awkward nakedness.

'What?' Lasser said.

21

'Your father is dead,' Carella said. 'He was killed some time this afternoon.'

'How?' Lasser asked. 'Was he in an accident of some ki . . .'

'No, he was murdered,' Carella said.

'Dead for a ducat,' the old woman said, and giggled.

Lasser's face was troubled now. He glanced first at the woman who seemed not to have grasped the meaning of Carella's words at all, and then he looked again at the detectives and said, 'Won't you come in, please?'

'Thank you,' Carella said, and he moved past the old woman who stood rooted in the doorway, staring at something across the street, staring so hard that Carella turned to look over his shoulder. He saw that Hawes was also staring across the street to where a small boy on a tricycle moved rapidly up the driveway to his house, a Tudor reproduction almost identical to the Lasser house.

'The king is dead,' the old woman said. 'Long live the king.'

'Won't you come in with us, ma'am?' Carella asked.

'He rides well, that boy,' the woman answered. 'Has a good seat.'

'Do you mean the boy on the bicycle?' Hawes asked.

'My mother doesn't often make sense,' Lasser said from the gloom beyond the open door's circle of light. 'Won't you come in, please? Mother, will you join us?'

'That which God hath joined together,' the woman said, 'let no man put asunder.'

'Mrs Lasser,' Carella said, and stepped aside to let her pass. The woman looked at Carella with a combination of malevolence and invitation in her eyes, an anger that threatened dire violence, a sexuality that promised sheer delight. She moved past him and into the house, and he followed her and heard the door closing behind him and then the voices of Hawes and Lasser behind him as they moved deeper into the entrance foyer.

The house was out of *Great Expectations*, sired by *Dragonwyck*, from *Wuthering Heights* twice removed. There were no actual cobwebs clinging to the ceilings and walls, but there was a feeling of foreboding gloom, a darkness that seemed permanently stained into the wooden beams and plaster, a certain knowledge that Dr Frankenstein or some damn ghoul was up in the attic working on God knew what foul creation. For a moment, Carella had the feeling he had stepped into the wrong horror movie, and he stopped deliberately and waited for Hawes to join him, not because he was frightened – well, the place *was* a bit eerie, but hell, hadn't he told young Mickey Ryan there was no such thing as ghosts? – but simply to reassure himself that he was really *here* inside this gloomy Tudor cottage investigating a murder which had taken place many miles away within the confines of the 87th Precinct where life was real and earnest, and so was death.

'I'll put on a light,' Lasser said, and he moved to a standing floor lamp behind a huge and ornate couch, snapped on the light, and then stood awkwardly beside the couch and his mother. Mrs Lasser stood with her hands entwined at her waist, a simpering smile on her lips, as though she were a Southern belle waiting to be asked for a dance at the yearly cotillion.

'Sit down, please,' Lasser said, and Carella searched for a chair and then sat on the couch. Hawes sat in a straight-backed chair which he pulled over from a drop-leaf desk against one wall. Mrs Lasser stood against that wall, smiling, still waiting to be asked for a dance. Lasser himself sat next to Carella on the couch.

'Can you tell us what happened?' Lasser said.

'Someone killed him with an axe,' Carella said.

'An axe?'

'Yes.'

'Where?'

'In the basement of the building where he works.'

'Why?' Lasser asked.

'Y is a crooked letter,' Mrs Lasser said, 'and A is for axe.'

'Mother, please,' Lasser said. He did not turn to face his mother as he said the words. His eyes did not even flick in her direction. It was as though he had said these same words a thousand times before, 'Mother, please,' and said them only unconsciously now, with no need to look at her or to face her, without even the need to know for certain that she had heard him. Still watching Carella, he said, 'Do you have any idea who might have done this?'

'None at all,' Carella said. 'Yet.'

'I see.'

'If you will, Mr Lasser, we'd like you to come down to the

morgue with us and make a positive identification. Then we'd like to know from you whether or not your father had any . . .'

'I couldn't leave my mother alone,' Lasser said.

'We could arrange for a patrolman to stay with her.'

'No, I'm afraid that would be unsatisfactory.'

'I don't understand, sir.'

'Either my father or I must stay with her at all times,' Lasser said. 'And since my father is dead, the burden is now mine.'

'I still don't understand,' Carella said. 'Even when your father was alive, he went to work in the city.'

'That's right,' Lasser said.

'Don't *you* work, Mr Lasser?'

'I work here,' Lasser said. 'At home.'

'Doing what?'

'I illustrate children's books.'

'I see. Then you were able to stay here at home whenever your father was gone, is that right?'

'Yes, that's right.'

'And whenever *he* was here, *you* were free to go, is that also correct?'

'Well, essentially, yes.'

'What I mean is, well, if you had a book to deliver, or an editorial conference, anything like that. Or a social engagement.'

'Essentially, that's it, yes.'

'Would you amend it in some way, Mr Lasser?'

'No.'

'Or correct it?'

'No. Essentially, that's it.'

'The word "essentially" implies that I haven't understood the complete picture,' Carella said. 'Could you fill me in on it, Mr Lasser?'

'Well . . .'

'Yes?'

'Well, I rarely leave the house,' Lasser said.

'What do you mean?'

'To deliver books. I do that by mail. Or for editorial conferences. I do that by phone. Anyway, I illustrate, as I told you, and there's not very much to discuss once the initial sketches have been submitted and approved.'

24

'But you do leave the house on social engagements?'

'Well, not very often.'

Carella was silent for a moment. Then he said, 'Mr Lasser, do you *ever* leave the house?'

'No,' Lasser answered.

'Are you agoraphobic, Mr Lasser?'

'Am I what?'

'Agoraphobic.'

'I don't know what that is.'

'Agoraphobia is an abnormal fear of going outdoors.'

'I'm not afraid of going outdoors,' Lasser said. 'Abnormally or otherwise.'

'When was the last time you went out, can you tell me that?'

'I don't remember.'

'You spend all of your time here in this house, is that right? With your mother.'

'And with my father, when he was alive.'

'You have your friends come here to see you, is that it?'

'Well, essentially, yes, that's it.'

'Again we have the "essentially", Mr Lasser.'

'Yes, well, the truth is my friends don't come here very often,' Lasser said.

'How often *do* they come, Mr Lasser?' Hawes asked.

'Not very often.'

'How often?'

'Never,' Lasser said. He paused. 'As a matter of fact, I don't *have* many friends.' He paused again. 'My books are my friends.'

'I see,' Carella said. He paused. 'Mr Lasser, would you be willing to identify the corpse from a photograph?'

'I have no objections.'

'We usually prefer a positive identification from the body . . .'

'Yes, but that's impossible, as you can see,' Lasser said. 'I must stay here with my mother.'

'Yes. With your permission then, we'll come back with the police photographs and perhaps you'd be so kind as to . . .'

'Yes.'

'And at that time,' Carella said, 'we'd also like to ask you some questions about your father and his personal relationships with other people.'

25

'Yes, of course.'

'But we won't burden you with that now,' Carella said, and he smiled.

'Thank you. I appreciate your consideration.'

'Not at all,' Carella said. He turned to the old woman. 'Good afternoon, Mrs Lasser.'

'God b'wi'you, and keep you, and heal your pate,' Mrs Lasser said.

'Ma'am?' Carella said.

'My mother used to be an actress. Those lines are from *Lear*.'

'*Henry the Fifth*,' the old lady corrected. 'Fluellen to Ancient Pistol.'

'Doth fortune play the huswife with me now?' Hawes said suddenly. 'News have I, that my Nell is dead i' th' spital of malady of France; and there my rendezvous is quite cut off.'

'How do you know that?' the old lady asked, turning to Hawes and grinning with delight.

'We did it in high school,' Hawes said.

'Who'd you play?'

'Nobody. I stage-managed.'

'A big man like you,' the old lady said. 'You should have been on the stage showing your cock.'

For a moment, there was a deep silence in the room. The detectives glanced at each other as though not certain they had heard the old lady's words. And then Anthony Lasser said, without turning to look at her, 'Mother, please,' and showed the detectives to the door. Behind them, they could hear Mrs Lasser laughing raucously. The door closed. They stood on the slate walk for a moment. It was late afternoon, and there was a new chill on the air. They lifted the collars of their coats, and listened to the sounds of the boy across the street as he pedalled his tricycle on the pavement and fired an imaginary pistol, 'P-kuh, p-kuh, p-kuh!'

'Let's go talk to him,' Carella said.

'Why?'

'I don't know.' He shrugged. 'The old lady was staring at him.'

'The old lady is nuts,' Hawes said.

'Mmm, that's for sure. What did you think of the son?'

'I don't know. He could be providing himself with an alibi a mile long.'

'Which is why I was jumping on him.'

'I know.'

'Or, on the other hand, he could be telling the truth.'

'I wish we knew a little more about the old man,' Hawes said.

'All in due time. When we come back with the pictures, we'll ask our questions.'

'While the corpse grows cold.'

'The corpse *is* cold,' Carella said.

'So's the case.'

'What can you do? It's January,' Carella answered, and they crossed the street.

The boy on the tricycle fired at them as they approached, 'P-kuh, p-kuh, p-kuh,' and then braked to a stop, his soles scraping along the pavement. He was perhaps four years old, wearing a red and white stocking cap pulled down over his ears. A hank of red hair stuck out of the cap's front and hung onto his forehead. His nose was running, and his face was streaked with dried mucus where he had repeatedly wiped his nose with the back of his hand.

'Hi,' Carella said.

'Who're you?' the boy asked.

'Steve Carella. Who're you?'

'Manny Moscowitz,' the boy said.

'Hi, Manny. This is my partner, Cotton Hawes.'

'Hi,' Manny said, and waved.

'How old are you, Manny?' Hawes asked.

'This many,' the boy said, and held up four fingers.

'Four years old. That's very good.'

'Five,' Manny said.

'No, that was four.'

'It was *five*,' Manny insisted.

'Okay, okay,' Hawes said.

'You don't know how to deal with kids,' Carella said. 'You're five, right, Manny?'

'Right,' Manny said.

'How do you like it around here?'

'Fine.'

'Do you live in this house right here?'

'Yeah.'

'Do you know the old lady across the street?'

27

'What old lady?'

'The one across the street,' Carella said.

'Which one across the street? There's lots of old ladies across the street.'

'Well, the one right in the house there,' Carella said.

'Which house?'

'Right there,' Carella said. He did not want to point because he had the certain feeling that Anthony Lasser was watching him from behind his drawn drapes.

'I don't know which house you mean,' Manny said.

Carella looked across the street at the identical Tudor reproductions, and then he sighed.

'He means, do you know Mrs Lasser?' Hawes asked, coming to his rescue.

'That's right,' Carella said. 'Do you know Mrs Lasser?'

'Is she the one in the house across the street?'

'Yes,' Carella said.

'Which house?' Manny asked, and a voice shouted, 'Manny! What are you doing there?'

Even before he turned, Carella knew it was another mother. There were days when all you got were mothers, sane or otherwise, and he knew without doubt that this was another mother, and he braced himself and turned just as the woman in a housedress with an open coat thrown over it, her hair in curlers, came marching down the front walk like a chowder society on Pennsylvania Avenue during Easter Week.

'What is it?' she said to Carella.

'How do you do, ma'am?' Carella said. 'I'm a police detective, we were simply asking your son some questions.'

'What kind of questions?'

'Oh, about the neighbourhood in general.'

'Did you just come from the Lasser house across the street?' the woman asked.

'Yes, ma'am.'

'Have you had complaints, is that it?'

'No, no complaints,' Carella said. He paused. 'Why do you say that, Mrs Moscowitz? You are Mrs Moscowitz?'

'Yes.' She shrugged. 'I just thought maybe you'd had some complaints. I thought maybe they were going to put the old lady away.'

28

'No, not that we know of. Why? Has there been any trouble?'

'Well, you know,' Mrs Moscowitz said. 'You hear stories.'

'What kind of stories?'

'Oh, you know. The husband a janitor someplace in the city, and he goes out every Sunday chopping down trees, God knows where he chops them, and carries them in to sell to his tenants, some funny business there, don't you think? And the old lady laughing half the night away and crying if her husband doesn't buy her an ice cream pop in the summer when the Good Humor truck comes around, that's peculiar, isn't it? And how about the son, Anthony? Drawing his pictures all day long in that back room overlooking the garden, summer and winter, and never stepping outside the house. I call that strange, mister.'

'He never goes out, you say?'

'Never. He's a shut-in. He's a regular shut-in.'

'*Who's* a shut-in?' the boy asked.

'Shut up, Manny,' his mother said.

'Anyway, what *is* a shut-in?' he asked.

'Shut up, Manny,' his mother said.

'You're sure he never goes out?' Carella asked.

'I've never seen him go out. Listen, how do I know what he does when it's dark? He may sneak out and go to opium dens, who knows? I'm only telling you that I, personally, have never seen him leaving the house.'

'What can you tell us about the old man?' Hawes asked.

'Mr Lasser?'

'Yes.'

'Well, now there's another peculiar thing, I mean besides his going out to chop down trees. I mean, this man is eighty-seven years old, you follow? That's not exactly a young teen-ager. But every Saturday and Sunday, out he goes to chop down his trees.'

'Does he take an axe with him?'

'An axe? No, no, he has one of those saws, what do you call them?'

'A chain saw?' Hawes suggested.

'Yes, that's right,' Mrs Moscowitz said. 'Even so, even with that saw, cutting down trees is very strenuous work for a man of eighty-seven years of age, am I right?'

'Absolutely,' Carella said.

'Certainly, but this isn't where it ends. Now mind you, there are hearty specimens in the world, I've seen men – well, my own father, may he rest in peace, he weighed a hundred and eighty pounds, all muscle, God bless him, when he died aged seventy-nine. But Mr Lasser is *not* a hearty specimen. Mr Lasser is a frail old man, but he is always doing very heavy work. Moving big rocks out of his back yard, and pulling up stumps, and painting the house, well, that's not very heavy work, but still, an old man like him on a ladder, to me it's very peculiar.'

'In other words, then, you feel the entire family is peculiar, is that right, Mrs Moscowitz?'

'I wouldn't say anything against neighbours,' Mrs Moscowitz said. 'Let's put it this way. Let's say I consider it odd, well, strange, well, let's say *peculiar*, all right? Let's say I find it peculiar that a nutty old lady like Mrs Lasser is left in the hands of two other nuts like her husband and her son, okay? Which is why I thought maybe somebody was going to have her put away, is all I'm saying.'

'Who's nutty?' the boy asked.

'Shut up, Manny,' Mrs Moscowitz said.

'Mrs Moscowitz,' Carella said, 'can you tell us whether or not you saw Anthony Lasser leaving the house at any time today?'

'No, I did not,' Mrs Moscowitz said.

'Can you say with certainty that he was inside that house all day long?'

'What?'

'Did you actually *see* him across the street at any time today?'

'No, I did not.'

'Then he could have been gone, without your knowing it?'

'Well, what do you think I do?' Mrs Moscowitz asked. 'Go peeking over my neighbours' window sills?'

'No, of course not.'

'I should *hope* not,' Mrs Moscowitz said, offended.

'We were simply trying to . . .'

'Yes, I understand,' Mrs Moscowitz said. 'Come along, Manny. Say good-bye to the two gentlemen.'

'Good-bye,' Manny said.

'Good-bye,' Carella answered. 'Thank you very much, Mrs Moscowitz.'

Mrs Moscowitz did not answer. With one hand on the handlebar of her son's bike, she led bike and child up the walk and into the house, and then slammed the door.

'What did I do?' Carella asked.

'I don't know how to handle kids, huh?'

'Well . . .'

'You don't know how to handle women,' Hawes said.

three

The woman's name was Teddy Carella, and she was his wife, and he knew how to handle her.

The positive identification had been made from photographs of the dead man by five-thirty that afternoon, after which Carella and Hawes had further questioned Anthony Lasser about his father, and then gone back to the squadroom to sign out. They left the station house at six-fifteen, a half-hour later than they should have, said good-bye on the precinct steps and headed off in opposite directions. Hawes had a date with a girl named Christine Maxwell. Carella had a date with his wife and two children.

His wife had black hair and brown eyes and a figure even the bearing of twins had failed to intimidate. Full-breasted, wide-hipped, long-legged, she greeted him in the foyer with a sound kiss and a hug that almost cracked his spine.

'Hey!' he said. 'Wow! What's going on?'

Teddy Carella watched his lips as he spoke because she was deaf and could hear only by watching a person's lips or hands. Then, because she was mute as well, she raised her right hand and quickly told him in the universal language of deaf mutes that the twins had already been fed and that Fanny, their housekeeper, was at this moment putting them to bed. Carella watched her moving hand, missing a word every now and then, but understanding the sense and meaning, and then smiled as she went on to outline her plans for the evening, as if her plans needed outlining after the kiss she had given him at the front door.

'You can get arrested for using that kind of language,' Carella said, grinning. 'It's a good thing everybody can't read it.'

Teddy glanced over her shoulder to make sure the door to the twins' room was closed, and then put her arms around his neck again and moved as close to him as it was possible to get and kissed him once again, and he almost forgot that it was his custom to go in to say good-night to the twins before he had his dinner.

'Well, I don't know what brought this on,' he said, and he raised one eyebrow appreciatively, and Teddy moved the fingers on her right hand rapidly and told him never to look a gift horse in the mouth.

'You're the nicest looking gift horse I've seen all week,' he said. He kissed the tip of her nose, and then went down the hall to the twins' room, knocking on the door before he entered. Fanny looked up from Mark's bed where she was tucking him in.

'Well, if it isn't himself,' she said, 'and knocking on doors in his own house.'

'My dear young lady . . .' Carella started.

'Young lady, is it? My, but he's in a good mood.'

'My, but he's in a good mood,' April echoed from her bed.

'My dear young lady,' Carella said to Fanny, 'if a person expects children to knock on *his* door before entering, he must set the proper example by knocking on *their* door before entering. Right, Mark?'

'Right, Pop,' Mark said.

'April?'

'Right, right,' April said, and giggled.

'Now don't get them all excited before bedtime,' Fanny warned.

Fanny who was in her fifties, red-haired and buxom, as Irish as Mrs Flannagan's underdrawers, turned from Mark's bed with a mock scowl on her face, kissed April perfunctorily and said, 'I'll leave you kiddies now to your horrid old man who will tell you tales of criminal deduction.'

'One day,' Carella said to the air, 'Fanny will marry someone and leave us, and all the humour will go out of our lives, and our house will be gloomy and sad.'

'Fat chance,' Fanny said, and grinned and went out of the room. She poked her head back around the door-jamb immediately and said, 'Dinner in five minutes. Make it snappy, Sherlock.'

32

'Who's Sherlock?' Mark asked.

'A cop,' Carella answered.

'Better than you?' Mark asked.

April scambled out of her bed, peeked at the open door to make sure Fanny wasn't coming back again, and then crawled into Carella's lap where he was sitting on the edge of Mark's bed. 'There's no cop better than Daddy,' she told her brother. 'Isn't that right, Daddy?'

Carella, not wishing to destroy a father image, modestly said, 'That's right, honey. I'm the best cop in the world.'

'Sure he is,' April said.

'I didn't say he *wasn't*,' Mark answered. 'She's always twisting it, Pop.'

'Don't call him Pop,' April said. 'His name is Daddy.'

'His name is Steve, smarthead,' Mark said.

'If you two are going to argue,' Carella said, 'I'll just leave.'

'She busted two of my models today,' Mark said.

'Why'd you do that, April?' Carella asked.

'Because he said I was a smarthead wetpants.'

'She is.'

'I didn't wet my pants all week,' April said.

'You wet them last night,' Mark corrected.

'I don't think that's any of your concern, Mark,' Carella said. 'What your sister does . . .'

'Sure, Pop,' Mark said. 'All I'm saying is she's a smarthead wetpants.'

'And I don't like that kind of language,' Carella said.

'What language?'

'Wetpants, he means,' April said.

'Why? What's wrong with that, Pop?'

'He only calls you Pop because he thinks that's tough,' April said. 'He's always trying to be a tough guy, Daddy.'

'I am not. Anyway, there's nothing wrong with being tough. Pop's tough, isn't he?'

'No,' April answered. 'He's very nice and sweet,' and she put her head against his chest and smiled. He looked down at her face, the dark black hair and brown eyes that were Teddy's, the widow's peak clearly defined even at the age of five, and then glanced at his son, amazed again by their absolute similarity and yet their total difference. There was no question that they were twins and therefore something more than simply brother and sister – their colouring was identical, the shapes of their faces, even the expressions they wore. But somehow April had managed to inherit – thank God – the beauty that was Teddy's, and Mark had retained this beauty only as a subtle undercoating to a façade that was more closely patterned after his father's.

'What'd you do today?' Mark asked, and Carella smiled and said, 'Oh, the same old thing.'

'Tell us, Daddy,' April said.

'No, you tell me what you did instead.'

'I busted two of Mark's models,' April said, and giggled.

'See, Pop? What'd I tell you?'

'Dinner!' Fanny called from the kitchen.

Carella rose with April in his arms, and then swung her out to plop her onto her own bed. He pulled the blanket to her chin and said, 'January night, sleep tight,' and kissed her on the forehead.

'What's that, Daddy?' April said.

'What's what, honey?'

'January night, sleep tight.'

'I just made it up,' Carella said.

He went to Mark's bed, and Mark said, 'Make up another one.'

'All's warm, all's dark,' Carella said. 'Sleep tight, dear Mark.'

'That's nice,' Mark said, smiling.

'You didn't make one with my name in it,' April said.

'Because I couldn't think of anything that rhymes with April,' Carella answered.

'You thought of something that could rhyme with Mark.'

'Well, Mark is easy, honey. April is very difficult to find a rhyme for.'

'Will you find one for it?'

'I'll try, honey.'

'Will you promise?' April asked.

'Yes, I promise,' he said. He kissed Mark and pulled the blanket to his chin.

'No, just under my nose,' Mark said.

'Okay. Here we go.' He pulled the blanket higher.

'Just under my nose, too, Daddy,' April said.

He tugged on her blanket, kissed her again, put out the light and went into the kitchen.

'What rhymes with April?' he asked Fanny.

'Don't bother me with your riddles,' Fanny said. 'Go sit down before your soup gets cold.'

During dinner, he told Teddy about the old man they had found in the basement. She watched his mouth as he spoke, stopping him every so often to ask a question, but for the most part simply watching him intently and trying to understand everything he said, listening carefully for details. She knew her husband very well, and she knew that this was not the last she would hear of the old man who had been slain with an axe. She knew there were husbands who left their work in the office, and she knew that her own husband had vowed a hundred times or more never to bring the sometimes filthy details of police work into his home. But each time his resolve would last a week, ten days, two weeks at the most, and suddenly he would begin talking about a particularly disturbing case, and always she would listen carefully. She listened because he was her husband, and she was his wife, and if he'd happened to be in the peanut industry, she would have listened to facts and figures about peanut oil and peanut butter.

Her husband's line of work was criminal detection.

So she listened to him as he talked about an eighty-seven-year-old man who had been found in the basement of a building with an axe in his head, and she listened as he told her of all the mother-son combinations he had met that day, listened as he told her of the demented Mrs Lasser and her son who never left the house, told her of the positive identification from a police photograph, told her of the way Mrs Lasser had begun laughing hysterically when she looked at the glossy identification photo of her dead husband, the axe still protruding from his skull, told her what Anthony Lasser had said about his father's friends, a group of Spanish-American War veterans who called themselves The Happy Kids. She listened with her eyes and her entire face. She asked questions with her silent lips and her rapidly moving hands.

Later, when the meal was finished, and the dishes were done, and the twins were sound asleep, and Fanny had left the house for the night, they went into their bedroom and stopped talking.

* * *

January 4th was a Saturday, but police departments do not know Saturday from Tuesday, nor for that matter Christmas from St Swithin's Day. Carella met Hawes at eight-thirty in the morning, and together they drove again to New Essex where they hoped to talk to some of the members of the late George Nelson Lasser's club, the group of Spanish-American War veterans who were known as The Happy Kids. The day was as bleak and foreboding as the day before had been. Carella was driving one of the squad's battered sedans, and Hawes seemed only half-awake on the seat beside him.

'Get in late last night?' Carella asked.

'No, not too late. We went to a movie.'

'What'd you see?'

'*The Locusts*,' Hawes said.

'Oh, yeah? How was it?'

'Well, it made me kind of itchy,' Hawes said. 'It's about these locusts that start an uprising, you know. Against the human race.'

'Why do they do that?'

'Well, that's a good question,' Hawes said. 'In fact, the Hero is asked that question about six or seven times in the picture, but all he can say each time is "I wish I knew". I'll tell you the truth, Steve, I wish *I* knew, too. All those locusts crawling all over everybody without any reason. It was very scary.'

'They just decide to kill humans, is that it?'

'Yeah. Well, there's a story besides. I mean, it isn't all about locusts killing people. There's a love story, too. Sort of.'

'What was the love story about?'

'Well, it's sort of about this girl who gives the hero two crickets in a cage. For his hearth, you see. You know, crickets on the hearth.'

'Yeah,' Carella said.

'Yeah, they make a pun about it, in fact. Instead of hearth, they say heart. Crickets on the heart.'

'That's pretty funny,' Carella said.

'Yeah,' Hawes said. 'So she follows this guy all the way to Pyongyang Province . . .'

'To where . . .?'

'Pyongyang Province. That's in Communist China.'

'Oh, I see.'

'Yeah, she follows him there with the crickets in the cage,

36

which he wanted as a gift for his aging Chinese nanny. She's very old, she's played by this woman who usually plays old Russian ladies, I forget her name. Anyway, that's why he wants these crickets, it's a little complicated.'

'Yeah,' Carella said.

'Christine thought it was the crickets who were the ring-leaders.'

'Of the locusts?'

'Yeah.'

'Maybe so,' Carella said.

'You think so? How could crickets communicate with locusts?'

'I'm not sure. How do they communicate with each other?'

'They rub their front legs together, I think.'

'Maybe it's the same with locusts.'

'I don't think the crickets had anything to do with it,' Hawes said. 'I think they were just a plot device. To get her to China.'

'Why'd they have to get her to China?'

'Well, hell, that's where all the locusts *are*, Steve. Also, it gave them a chance to bring in a very pretty Chinese girl, what's her name, you know her, she's in all the things where they need a Chinese girl. She turns out to be an old girlfriend of the hero's, she's teaching in a Catholic mission which the locusts attack near the end of the picture. They eat the priest.'

'What?'

'Yeah,' Hawes said.

'That sounds like some picture.'

'Yeah, it was. They didn't show him being eaten, of course. But the locusts were all over him, chewing.'

'Yeah,' Carella said.

'Yeah. They had some nice closeups.'

'Who was the girl?'

'Some new girl, I forget her name.'

'And the hero?'

'Oh, he's been around on television. I forget his name, too.' Hawes hesitated. 'Actually, the locusts were the stars of the picture.'

'Yeah,' Carella said.

'Yeah. They had one scene where there must have been eight million locusts hopping all over everybody. I wonder how they got that scene.'

'There probably was a locust trainer,' Carella said.

'Oh, sure.'

'I saw a picture called *The Ants* once,' Carella said.

'How was it?'

'Pretty good. It sounds a little like *The Locusts*, though there wasn't the girl bringing any crickets in a cage.'

'No, huh?'

'No. There was a girl, but she was a newspaper reporter investigating this nuclear reactor that blows up out in the country someplace. That's what makes the ants get so big.'

'Oh, they were bigger than normal ants, you mean?'

'Sure.'

'Oh, well these locusts were their normal size. I mean, there wasn't any funny stuff with nuclear reactors or anything like that?'

'No, these were big ants,' Carella said.

'*The Ants*, huh? That was the name of the picture?'

'Yeah, *The Ants*.'

'This one was called *The Locusts*,' Hawes said.

'*The Locusts*.'

'Yeah.'

They drove in silence into the heart of town. They had been told the day before that The Happy Kids met in a vacant store on East Bond – Lasser could not remember the address. They searched the street now for the store, which they had also been told was unmarked. They found what seemed to be an empty store in the middle of the 300 block, curtained across its door and its wide plate glass windows. Carella parked the car across the street, pulled down the sun visor to which was affixed a hand-lettered sign advising the New Essex Police that this antiquated heap was driven by a city detective on a duty call, and then joined Hawes who came around the car and fell into step beside him.

They tried to see over the curtains on the front windows, but found that they were hung on rods above their line of vision. Hawes went to the front door and tried it. It was locked.

'What do we do?' he asked. 'I don't see a bell, do you?'

'No. Why don't you rap on the glass?'

'I'm afraid I'll wake up all the gypsies,' Hawes said.

'Try it.'

Hawes rapped on the glass. He looked at Carella, waiting. He rapped again. He took the door handle and shook the door. 'Anybody in there?' he shouted.

'Don't take it off the hinges,' a voice said.

'Ah-ha,' Carella said.

'Who is it?' the voice behind the door asked.

'Police,' Hawes said.

'What do you want?' the voice asked.

'We want to talk to The Happy Kids,' Hawes said.

'Just a minute,' the voice answered.

'That sounded stupid as hell,' Hawes whispered to Carella, and the door opened. The man standing in the door-frame was perhaps ninety years old, give or take a few centuries. He leaned on his cane and peered out at the detectives malevolently, wheezing air into his sunken chest, his mouth twitching, his eyes blinking.

'Let's see it,' he snapped.

'See what, sir?' Carella said.

'Your identification.'

Carella opened his wallet to his shield. The old man studied it and then said, 'You're not New Essex police?'

'No, sir.'

'Didn't think so,' the old man said. 'What is it you want?'

'George Lasser was murdered yesterday,' Carella said. 'We understand he belonged to . . .'

'What? What did you say?'

'I said George Lasser . . .'

'Mister, don't joke with an old man.'

'We're not joking, sir,' Carella said. 'Mr Lasser was murdered yesterday afternoon.'

The old man in the door digested this silently for several moments, then nodded his head, and then sighed, and then said, 'My name is Peter Maily. Come in.'

The store was furnished much as Carella had imagined it would be. There was a huge, black, pot-bellied stove against one wall, and over it some regimental flags and a group picture of some battle-weary soldiers taken just outside El Canay. A dilapidated couch was against the wall opposite the stove, and several stuffed and decaying easy chairs were scattered around the room. A television set was going in one corner, watched by two

39

gloomy old men who barely glanced up as Hawes and Carella came into the room. If Peter Maily and these two others were The Happy Kids, they seemed to dispense a particular brand of somnolent gloom which was uniquely and exclusively their own. If ever there was a club that seemed singularly unclubby, this was it. Carella was certain that a smile on these premises would mean immediate expulsion from the group.

'You *are* The Happy Kids?' he asked Maily.

'Oh, yes, we're The Happy Kids, all right,' Maily said. 'What's left of us.'

'And you *did* know George Lasser?'

'With us when we took Siboney and, later on, El Canay,' Maily said. 'Picture's up there on the wall, with the rest of us.' He turned to the men watching the television set and said, 'George's dead, fellers. Got it yesterday.'

A bald-headed old man wearing a checked weskit turned away from the set and said, 'How, Peter?'

Maily turned to Carella. 'How?' he asked.

'Someone hit him with an axe.'

'Who?' the man in the checked weskit asked.

'We don't know.'

The other man at the television set, straining to hear the conversation, cupped his hand behind his ear and said, 'What is it, Frank?'

The man in the checked weskit said, 'Georgie's dead. Got killed with an axe. They don't know who done it, Fred.'

'Georgie's dead, did you say?'

'Yep, got killed with an axe.'

The other man nodded.

'We were wondering if you could tell us what you know about Mr Lasser?' Carella said. 'Anything that might help us to find his murderer.'

'Be happy to,' the man named Frank said, and the interrogation began.

The man who had opened the door, Peter Maily, seemed to be president of the group, which now consisted of three members, himself and the two who'd been watching the television set. The two television watchers were called Frank Ostereich and Fred Nye. Ostereich was secretary of the group, and Nye was treasurer – all chiefs and no Indians, it seemed. There had, however, been

40

twenty-three Indians back in April of 1898. Or, to be more exact, there had been twenty-three youngsters who were all in their late teens or early twenties, and they were members of a New Essex social and athletic club called The Happy Kids. It being 1898, there was no juvenile delinquency and therefore the term 'social and athletic club' was not a euphemism for 'bopping gang'. These happy kids actually had a baseball team and a volley ball team and a rented store – this same store they now rented – on East Bond Street, in which they held dances every Friday night and sometimes necked with girls on weekday nights in the back room.

Well, in 1898, when the United States of America was suffering heavy economic losses in Cuba due to revolutions and guerilla warfare and garrisoned Spanish towns, when the United States was simultaneously beginning to feel its oats in the Western Hemisphere and recognizing the importance of Cuba to Central America where a canal was being planned, two things happened: William Randolph Hearst published a letter from a Spanish minister in Washington, D.C., written to a friend in Cuba and expressing contempt for President McKinley; and the United States battleship *Maine* was sunk in Havana harbour. Well, you know how it is with Cuba; one thing always leads to another. It wasn't until April 24th that Spain officially declared war, at which time the American Congress replied by stating the two countries had been at war since April 21st.

The Happy Kids enlisted as a group under W. S. Shafter and were part of the 17,000 U.S. troops who landed in Cuba and began a march on Santiago. Considering the fact that there had been twenty-three boys in the social and athletic club, considering also how badly trained and poorly equipped the troops were, it was something of a miracle that The Happy Kids all survived the heavy fighting at Siboney and El Canay. None of the group was killed and only one man was wounded, a boy named Billy Winslow who took a Spanish slug in his calf. The bullet embedded in his leg enabled him in later years to predict accurately the kind of weather that could be expected on any given day in New Essex and the surrounding towns. This stunt made him very popular with the ladies and earned the respect and admiration of a girl named Janice Terrill, one of the prettiest girls in town, who – it was reputed – allowed young Billy to remove her petticoat and

41

assorted sundry undergarments in the back room of the store one rainy afternoon he had predicted. They were married six months later.

As a matter of fact, of the twenty-three Happy Kids who survived the invasion of Cuba and the march through Siboney and El Canay, twenty were married by the turn of the century, and the remaining three – including George Nelson Lasser – were married shortly thereafter.

'What kind of a soldier was he?' Carella asked.

'Georgie? Same as the rest of us. Inexperienced, young, full of pepper. We're lucky we all didn't get our brains blown out.'

'What rank did he hold?'

'Private first class.'

'Did he come right back to New Essex after he was discharged?'

'Yes.'

'What did he do?'

'Odd jobs. I guess he was trying to make up his mind. He always was an ambitious fellow, Georgie. I guess that was why he married Estelle. That was in 1904. January it was, matter of fact. That's funny, isn't it?'

'How do you mean?' Hawes asked.

'Well,' Maily said, 'he was married in January of 1904, and here it is January again, sixty years later, and well, he's been killed. That's pretty funny.'

'Peter don't mean funny to laugh at,' Ostereich said. 'He means strange.'

'Yes, that's right,' Maily said. 'I mean strange.'

'What did George Lasser's ambition have to do with marrying the woman he did?' Carella asked.

'Estelle? Well, she was an actress, you know.'

'What was her full name?'

'Estelle Valentine,' Nye said. 'I think that was her stage name though. Isn't that right, Peter?'

'That's right,' Maily said. 'Matter of fact, I don't think I ever knew her real name.'

'A Russian name,' Ostereich said. 'She's a Russian, I think.'

'Have you ever met her?' Nye asked.

'Yes,' Carella said.

'Then you know she's crazy, huh?'

'She seemed . . . well . . .' Carella shrugged.

'Oh, she's nutty as a fruitcake, all right,' Ostereich said.

'*All* actresses are nutty,' Maily said.

'Yes, but she wasn't even a *good* actress,' Nye said. 'Good ones may have a right to be a little nuts, though I'm not even sure of that. But bad ones? No right at all.'

'I still don't see what marrying her had to do with ambition,' Carella said.

'Well, she must have seemed pretty important to Georgie. He met her when she came here to New Essex in *Captain Jinks of the Horse Marines*, do you know that one?'

'No,' Carella said.

'Probably before your time,' Maily said. 'Ethel Barrymore played it in 1901. Well, Estelle Valentine wasn't no Ethel Barrymore, believe me, but she came to New Essex anyway in a road company, must have opened here around Christmas of 1903, I guess, over at the New Essex Playhouse. It's a movie theatre now, everything changes. Georgie fell in love with her right off. She was a pretty little thing, I got to admit that. They got married . . . well, almost immediately.'

'Sixty years ago,' Carella said.

'Yes, that's right.'

'The son seems to be in his forties,' Carella said.

'Tony Lasser? Yes, that's right. He came late. Neither of the two wanted children. Estelle always talked about going back to the stage and Georgie always had his big plans. Tony came as something of a surprise. They were neither of them exactly grassy green when he was born. You ask me, that's what finally sent Estelle off her rocker.'

'There's something I don't understand,' Carella said.

'What's that?'

'George Lasser was a janitor.'

'That's right,' Maily said.

'These ambitions you keep talking about, these plans of his . . .'

'Oh, don't think Estelle didn't throw that up to him all the time,' Ostereich said, 'You know, the old baloney. I gave up my career for you, and what did I get in return? A janitor!'

'Georgie always had things going for him, though,' Nye said. 'In the Army, he always had something to sell, either chickens he'd picked up in the farmhouse, or souvenir pistols or flags, always something. Once even, a string of whores he rounded up someplace,' Nye chuckled with the memory.

'Well, even when we got back here to town,' Ostereich said, 'how about that? The dances he used to run over at the Republican Club, and the boat rides he dreamt up. Georgie was always trying to think up ways to make a buck. Very ambitious, he was.'

'But then he became a janitor, right?' Carella said. 'He forgot all about his ambitions, is that it?'

'Actually, he was more than just a janitor,' Maily said.

'Yes? What was he?' Carella asked.

'Well, what I mean to say is that he still had other little things going for him.'

'Like what?'

'Like the wood. He used to go out cutting trees here in the woods, and carry them into the city in his truck. Then he got some coloured fellow to chop them up for him, and he sold them to the tenants in his building, turned a pretty penny that way.'

'What else did he have going for him?' Carella asked.

'Well . . .' Maily said.

'Yes?'

'Well, just the wood, that's all,' Maily said, and he glanced at the other men.

'Sir, what else did George Lasser have going for him?'

'Nothing,' Maily said.

'You said he was an ambitious man.'

'Yes, because of the wood,' Maily said. 'Because of his selling the wood. That was very ambitious. After all, he was an old man. Not every man his age would . . .'

'Sir,' Carella said, 'if I heard you correctly, you told us that George Lasser was more than just a janitor and you said he had other little *things* going for him. You said *things*, sir. Plural. Now what else did he have going for him besides the wood business?'

'Well, being the super of the building is all I meant. I meant that and the wood business.'

'I think you're lying, sir,' Carella said, and the store went silent. Carella waited.

'We're old men,' Maily said at last.

'I know that, sir.'

'We're old men waiting to die. We came through a war together long ago, and back to New Essex together, and we went

44

to each other's weddings and when we began to have kids, we went to baptisms and communions and barmitzvahs, and we even went to the weddings of the kids, and are halfway to seeing *their* kids grown up and married, too. We're old men, Mr Carella.'

'Yes, sir, I know that. I want to know about George Lasser.'

'What we go to now, Mr Carella, is funerals. That's what we go to now. No more weddings. Only funerals. Twenty-three of us in the beginning. The Happy Kids. And now there are three of us left, and all we go to are funerals.'

'George Lasser didn't have an enemy in the world,' Ostereich said.

'He shouldn't have died like that,' Nye said. 'Not this way.'

'Leave him be,' Maily said to Carella. 'He's dead. Let us bury him the way we buried all the others. Let him rest in peace.'

'I'm waiting, Mr Maily,' Carella said.

Maily sighed. He glanced at Ostereich. Ostereich gave a small nod, and Maily sighed again.

'George Lasser used to run a crap game in the basement of his building,' he said.

four

Danny Gimp was a stool pigeon; and as an informer, he felt that the American aversion to rats was part of a conspiracy begun in elementary school and designed to deprive him of a profession at which he was a master. He had often thought of hiring a press agent or a public relations man to construct a more acceptable public image of himself, but he had the good sense to know the aversion was too deeply ingrained in the American spirit to be changed by a mere manipulator of images. He could not understand why people felt it was wrong to tell tales about other people. Nor could he understand why a largely law-abiding citizenry had adopted as one of its hidebound codes a precept that had originated in – and was strongly encouraged and enforced by – the underworld. He only knew that if a person saw someone doing something wrong, he was reluctant to go to the authorities with his information. And whereas Danny knew that part of this reluctance was caused by fear of reprisal, he further knew that most of the reluctance was caused by the code: Thou Shalt Not Tell.

Why not?

He enjoyed telling.

He was a gossip supreme, his ears keenly attuned to every stray piece of information that wafted his way on the unsuspecting air. His mind was a complex of compartments and cubbyholes, each storing kernels of seemingly worthless information which, when evaluated, added up to a meaningful fund of knowledge. He was an expert at sifting and sorting, collating and cataloguing, all tricks he had learned as a boy when a bout with polio had caused him to be bedridden for the better part of a year. When you can't leave the bedroom, you begin to think of ways to amuse yourself. Danny Gimp, considering his talent for amusing himself, might have become a banker and the mastermind behind an international cartel if he hadn't been born and raised on Culver Avenue, which was not one of the city's garden spots. Having been born on Culver Avenue, and giving the devil his due, he also might have become an international jewel thief, or – what is more likely – a pimp. He became neither. He became, instead, a stool pigeon.

His real name was Danny Nelson, but no one ever called him that. Even mail addressed to Danny Gimp was delivered to him by his faithful mailman who thought Danny was a World War I veteran who had been wounded in the Ardennes, rather than a stool pigeon. As a matter of fact, there were very few people who knew that Danny Gimp was a stool pigeon, it being a necessity in the profession to keep one's activities quiet, lest one discover one night that several hired guns were after one, objective homicide. Being chased by gangland torpedoes, very oldhat terminology for guns, is not entertaining even if you do not limp slightly. When you do limp, it is difficult to run very fast, so Danny decided it was best to avoid any friction between himself and either oldhat torpedoes *or* fashionable guns, thereby eliminating footraces through the city streets.

Danny told everybody he was a burglar.

This made him socially acceptable, and it also encouraged

other assorted thieves to open their hearts to him. Every time they opened their hearts, Danny opened the voluminous filing cabinets inside his skull and began collecting information, dropping bits and pieces into place here and there, making no attempt to evaluate, sorting and filing as he went along, hoping all of it would make better sense later.

A twenty-two-year-old hood might tell Danny that he needed a new rear tyre for a late model Oldsmobile, does Danny know a good fence? Danny does indeed know a fence – not a good one, actually; actually he has done time in at least three state prisons, so how good can he be? – and while he is asking the man about a tyre for his young friend, the fence casually mentions that a fur warehouse on Tenth Street was knocked over on Tuesday night, with the night watchman taking a slug in the forehead, unfortunately killing the old man. Danny clucks sympathetically, and the next day he sees his young friend's wife – who used to be a hooker but who has graduated to the big time since she now has a husband who can keep her in heroin – and lo and behold, the wife is swathed in what appears to be four hundred yards of natural let-out ranch mink. Danny has never known what 'let-out mink' meant, but he suspects that this particular mink was let out of that warehouse on Tenth Street by none other than his young friend who now needs a new right tyre for his late model Oldsmobile. He reads in the newspaper the next day that the nightwatchman must have got off a few shots at a retreating person or thing before his untimely demise, his service revolver having been found with only two bullets in it. When Danny sees his young friend he asks him how come he needs a new right rear tyre. His friend says, 'I picked up a nail on the parkway.' Danny looks at his friend and wonders why he doesn't simply go to a garage and have them repair the tyre, if all he picked up in it was a nail? There is the possibility, however, that the nail has really done big damage to the wheel, making it necessary to replace it. Danny is willing to give his friend the benefit of the doubt; after all, if replacement really is necessary, he knows his friend would automatically go to a fence for the merchandise.

Fences are the best discount houses in the city. They sell anything you might need, from Westinghouse portable television sets, to Smith and Wesson portable .38 revolvers, and at very good prices indeed. Even square citizens in bad neighbourhoods utilize the services of a fence, so why shouldn't a cheap hood like Danny's young friend, in dire need of a new tyre, go to a fence – even if there *isn't* anything suspicious about why he happens to need a new tyre?

A good stoolie never jumps to conclusions.

He collects, he sifts, he collates, he waits.

A week later, Danny runs across a fellow who has just come in from Chicago where he has been for several days. The fellow is carrying a very big bundle. That night, Danny sees the Chicago fellow and also his young hood friend riding around in the Oldsmobile together, the right rear tyre replaced by now. The next day, Danny's young hood friend is sporting a very big bundle, and the hood's wife is on a heroin-buying jag that will keep her stocked until China runs out of poppy flowers.

What Danny reports to the police is that he believes his young hood friend broke into the warehouse with his Chicago pal, was shot at by the night watchman who put a hole in their right rear tyre, and who received a hole in his forehead in return. He further tells the police that he believes the furs were dumped in Chicago and that the two thieves only recently split the cash received for the loot.

For his services, Danny gets ten bucks from the detective to whom he divulges this. The ten bucks comes out of a fund loosely described as 'petty cash'. Neither the detective nor Danny report this exchange on their income tax.

It was not at all surprising that very few people knew Danny was a stool pigeon since he could very easily have passed for a burglar or a mugger or a cheque passer, or any one of a number of criminal types, all of whom looked exactly the way Danny looked, which is to say they all looked like normal everyday human beings who were honest citizens. Except they happened to be crooks.

Danny didn't happen to be a crook. He was as honest as the day is long. He only *said* he was a crook.

He had, in fact, spent five years in a prison in California when he got convicted in a criminal case out there back in 1938. It was this prison stay which convinced everyone that Danny Gimp was indeed a practising burglar, especially since he told everyone he'd been serving a five and dime on a Burglary One conviction out there. This happened to be true. But actually, he'd only gone to Los Angeles for his health.

He had been bothered with a persistent cold and an accompanying low fever for perhaps two months when his family physician suggested that he go out to California to get some sun and some rest, away from his normal city pursuits. Danny had just helped the bulls of the Seventy-First to crack a particularly difficult whore house set-up, and the bulls (in tandem with some Vice Squad cops) were grateful to the tune of five hundred bucks for his assistance, mainly because five of them received promotions out of the crack-down. Danny, flush with his five hundred dollars, running this low fever and coughing all the time, went out to Los Angeles.

Ah, land of glamour and mystery, ah, city of sun and stars, ah, cultural citadel!

He got arrested four days after he arrived.

The way he got arrested was very peculiar since he had no idea he was committing a crime at the time. He met a fellow in a bar on La Brea and they began drinking and telling jokes and the man asked Danny what line of work he was in and Danny said, 'Communications'. The man thought this was very interesting because he himself was in a line of work he described as 'Redistribution' and they had a few more drinks and it was then that the man asked Danny to accompany him to his house where he wanted to pick up some more money so they could continue their fun and revelry, drinking and talking shop and laughing it up in good old L.A.

They drove up the Strip past La Cienega and then the man turned his car up into the hills and they pulled up in front of a good-looking Spanish-type hacienda house all stuccoed and tiled, and Danny and the man got out of the car and went up to the back door which the man opened. They didn't put on any lights because the man didn't want to wake his brother, he said, who was a manic-depressive and lived in the back room.

The very polite Los Angeles police, all of whom had studied under Joe Friday, picked up Danny and his friend as they were leaving the house. Danny's friend had not only taken several hundred dollars in cash from the bedroom of the house which (surprise!) was not his house at all – but he had also managed to pick up a diamond and ruby necklace which the police valued at forty-seven thousand five hundred dollars.

Ah, land of glamour and mystery, citadel of culture.

Danny told the judge he had met the fellow in a bar and had only accompanied him to his . . .

Sure, sure, the judge said.

. . . house there in the Santa Monica Mountains because the man wanted to . . .

Sure, sure, the judge said.

. . . pick up some money so they could continue their evening of fun and revelry, drinking and talking shop and . . .

Sure, sure.

. . . laughing it up in good old L.A.

A minimum of five and a maximum of ten, the judge said.

What? Danny said.

Next case, the judge said.

It wasn't too bad. Danny lost his cold in stir, and also his accompanying low fever. He learned in stir that a stool pigeon is called 'a snitch', a piece of juvenile terminology which convinced him more than ever that the code against informing began somewhere in the lower grades of school. He also derived from prison the single 'reference' that would be invaluable in his later working days. He could in the future, when talking to or listening to an assorted number of thieves, announce in all honesty that he had served a rap for burglary in a West Coast pen. Who then could possibly imagine that Danny Gimp was an informer, a stoolie, a rat, a tattletale, or even God forbid a snitch?

Steve Carella could.

He found Danny in the third booth on the right-hand side of the bar called Andy's Pub. Danny was not an alcoholic, nor did he even drink to excess. He simply used the bar as a sort of office. It was cheaper than paying rent downtown, and it had the added attraction of a phone booth which he used regularly. The bar, too, was a good place to listen – and listening was one-half of Danny's business.

Carella scanned the joint as he walked in, spotted Danny immediately in his customary booth, but also saw two known hoods sitting at the bar. He walked past Danny without so much as glancing at him, took a stool at the bar, and asked for a beer.

50

Since cops emit a smell which can be detected by certain individuals, usually lawbreakers, the way certain sounds can be detected only by dogs, the bartender gave Carella his beer and then asked, 'Anything wrong, officer?'

'Just felt like having a beer,' Carella said.

The bartender smiled sweetly and said, 'Then I take it this is an off-duty visit.'

'Mm-huh, that's right,' Carella said.

'Not that we have anything to hide here,' the bartender said, still smiling.

Carella didn't bother answering him. He finished his beer and was reaching into his pocket for his wallet when the bartender said, 'It's on the house, officer.'

'I'd rather pay for it, thanks,' Carella said.

The bartender didn't argue. He simply figured Carella was a cop who took bigger bribes. Carella paid for the beer, walked out of the bar without looking at Danny, pulled up his coat collar as he reached the street, walked two blocks downtown heading into a biting bitter wind, then turned and began walking uptown again on the opposite side of the street, with the wind at his back. He ducked into a doorway across the street from the bar and waited for Danny Gimp to come out. Danny, who was playing this a little too goddamn cool for a January day with a twenty-mile-an-hour wind blowing, did not come out of the bar until some ten minutes later. By that time, Carella's toes and nose were freezing. He slapped his gloved hands together, pulled his collar up once more, and began following Danny. He did not overtake him until the two had walked almost seven blocks, one behind the other. Falling into step beside Danny, he said, 'What the hell took you so long?'

'Hey, hi,' Danny said. 'You must be froze, huh?'

'This isn't exactly Miami Beach,' Carella said.

'Worse luck, huh?' Danny said. 'Did you happen to glom the pair at the bar?'

'Yeah.'

'You make them?'

'Sure. Ralph Andrucci and Pinky Deane.'

'Hey, that's right,' Danny said. 'Well, they made you, too. They spotted you for a bull right off, and they gave the bartender the eye to find out what you were doing there, and they didn't

51

buy none of that off-duty crap for a minute. So I figured it was better I stick around a little while instead of rushing right out here, you dig? Because, in my line, you got to be a little careful, you dig?'

'I dig,' Carella said.

'How come you didn't call?'

'I thought I'd take a chance.'

'I prefer that you call,' Danny said, seemingly offended. 'You know that.'

'Well, the truth of the matter is that I like hanging around on street corners when it's cold enough to freeze the balls off a brass monkey,' Carella said. 'That's why I stopped by and then went right outside to wait for you.'

'Oh, I see,' Danny said.

'Yeah.'

'Look, I'm sorry. I got to protect myself.'

'Next time I'll call,' Carella said.

'I'd appreciate it.'

They walked in silence for several blocks.

'What's on your mind?' Danny asked at last.

'A crap game,' Carella answered.

'Where?'

'4111 South Fifth. In the basement.'

'Regular or one-shot?'

'Regular.'

'Floating or stationary?'

'Stationary.'

'The same place each time?'

'Right.'

'Which is the basement of 4111 South Fifth, correct?'

'Correct,' Carella said.

'Which also happens to be where somebody got his head busted Friday, also correct?'

'Also correct,' Carella said.

'So what do you want to know?'

'Everything about it.'

'Like?'

'Who played and when? Who won and who lost?'

'What's the dead man's connection with the game?' Danny asked.

52

'He ran it.'

'What was his cut? Usual house cut?'

'I don't know. Find out for me.'

'You said this was a permanent game, huh? And the same place each time?'

'That's right.'

'You talked to your sergeant on the beat yet?'

'No.'

'You'd better.'

'Why?'

'Chances are he knew about it. He was probably cutting the pot along with Lasser.'

'Maybe. I'll get to him on Monday.'

'I've got to tell you . . .' Danny started.

'Yeah?'

'I haven't heard a word about this, not a peep. It's your notion somebody in the game chopped him down, is that it?'

'I don't have any notions yet, Danny. I'm fishing.'

'Yeah, but why fish around a crap game? Dice players don't usually go chopping a man down with an axe.'

'Where else do I fish?'

Danny shrugged. 'From what I read in the newspaper, Steve, it sounds like a nut.' He shrugged again. 'You got a nut? Go fishing around him.'

'I've got one. I've also got her son, who draws pictures and never leaves the house. And I've got three old cockuhs who survived the Spanish-American War and who are sitting around waiting to drop dead themselves any minute now. I've also got an underpaid Negro who knows how to use an axe, but I don't think he used it on our man.'

'And you've got a crap game.'

'Right. So where do I fish?'

'The crap game.'

'Sure,' Carella said. 'A crap game makes sense to me.'

'Don't lean too heavy,' Danny said. 'This might be a game full of guys from the building, they come down once, twice a week just to pass the time.'

'Could be, sure.'

'Or what it could be,' Danny said, 'is some nice retures and never leaves the house. And I've got three old night a week to

53

howl, they come shoot craps in a slum basement instead of drinking or chasing after dames.'

'Sure, that too,' Carella said. 'Or it could be a bunch of hoods who've got no place else to play and who give George Lasser a cut for letting them use his basement.'

'Mmm, maybe,' Danny said.

'In which case, an axe murder isn't so very far out, is it?'

'An axe murder is *always* very far out,' Danny said. 'You know any pro who'll use an axe? Impossible. You're dealing with Amateur Night, Steve. That's why I'm telling you not to lean so heavy on the crap game. I mean, even if the game was full of the worst hoods ever walked this city, who do you know's gonna use an axe on a guy?'

Carella looked suddenly troubled.

'What'd I do?' Danny asked. 'Screw it up for you?'

'No, no. But I'll tell you what I don't like about this crap game, Danny. It's against the law. That makes everybody in it a lawbreaker. And if they've all broken the law already . . .'

'Aw, come on, Steve,' Danny said. 'Gambling's a misdemeanour.'

'Even so.'

'So a dice player's gonna suddenly pick up an axe? And brain somebody with it? Aw, come on, Steve.'

'You don't buy it?' Carella asked.

Danny was quiet for a long time. Then he shrugged and said, 'Old Chinese saying: Play with dice like play with blonde. Man never get out what he put in.'

Carella smiled.

'So who knows?' Danny continued. 'Maybe there was a heavy loser in the game, and maybe he got himself an axe someplace . . .'

'In the shed behind the building,' Carella said.

'Sure, and decided Lasser was the one to blame for his bad luck. Pow, good-bye janitor.' Danny shrugged again. 'It could be. Guys go crazy over dice, the same like with a broad. But I don't figure it for a pro. A pro puts a bullet in the old guy's head, plain and simple. Or a shaft in his back. But an axe? I mean, Jesus, that's pretty disgusting, ain't it? An axe?'

'Will you listen around?' Carella asked.

'I'll get back,' Danny said. He paused. 'I'm short, you know.'

'So am I,' Carella said.

'Yeah, but I live dangerously.'

'I had to put in a new muffler,' Carella said.

'Huh?'

'On one of the squad sedans.'

'So? *You* had to pay for that?'

'Petty Cash had to pay for that?'

'Where does this "Petty Cash" come from, anyway?' Danny asked. 'Does the city honour your chits, or what?'

'We push dope on the side,' Carella answered.

'Listen, I'll believe you,' Danny said.

'When will you call me?'

'As soon as I've got something. Listen, Steve, no kidding, I'm real short. I could use some . . .'

'Danny, if *you* come up with something, *I'll* come up with something. I'm not stalling you. The cupboard is bare right now.'

'Boy oh boy,' Danny said, 'two bare cupboards in the middle of January. It's enough to make you quit police work, ain't it?' He grinned, glanced over his shoulder, shook hands with Carella briefly but firmly, and said, 'I'll give you a ring.'

Carella watched as he limped away. Then he put his gloved hands in his pockets and began walking the fifteen blocks back to where he had parked his car.

five

If you're a cop, you know all about graft.

You know that if somebody is taking, it is usually the senior man on the beat who later splits with the other men who share the beat on a rotating basis. You know this because you also know there is nothing that can screw things up like a plenitude of cops with outstretched hands. When too many hands are reaching, the sucker may suddenly decide that he is really being taken but good, and one fine day the desk sergeant will receive a call from someone who will say, simply, 'I want to talk to a detective.'

Sergeant Ralph Corey did not wish to talk to a detective.

This was Monday morning, and he was about to begin five consecutive tours on the 8.0 a.m. to 4.0 p.m. shift, after which he would swing for fifty-six hours and then come back to work on Sunday at midnight to begin his next five tours on the graveyard shift, from midnight to 8.0 a.m. The shift after that would be from 4.0 p.m. to midnight, and then the rotation would come full circle and he would be back on the day shift for the next five tours.

A police department is a small army. Even in a big army, you don't mess around with the sergeant. Corey was not only a sergeant and the senior man on his beat, he also happened to be the senior sergeant of all twelve sergeants in the precinct, with the exception of Dave Murchison. Murchison didn't count, though, since he handled the switchboard and the muster desk, and never walked a beat.

Sergeant Ralph Corey, then, was a V.I.P., a B.M.O.C., a *gonsuh mockuh*, a wheel, and a guy around whom you watched your onions.

There was only one trouble.

Steve Carella outranked him.

Steve Carella was, in this small army that was the police force, in this section of the army that was the 87th Precinct, a Detective 2nd/Grade – which is higher than a sergeant. It is two steps higher than a sergeant. Even if Carella had liked Corey, he would have outranked him. Since he didn't like him, he outranked him in spades. Corey looked like a big, red-faced stereotype of a mean, lousy cop; but in Corey's case, the stereotype was true. He *was* a mean cop and a lousy cop and the only reason he was a sergeant was that he'd shot an escaping bank robber purely by sheer dumb luck back in 1947. His gun had gone off accidentally as he'd pulled it out of his holster, that's how lucky Corey had been, and the bullet had taken the running thief in the left leg. So Corey had received a commendation and a promotion to Sergeant and had damn near made Detective/3rd to boot, but hadn't.

Carella hadn't liked him back in 1947, and he didn't like him now, but he smiled as Corey entered the squadroom and then said, 'Have a seat, Ralph. Cigarette?' and pushed his pack across the desk while Corey watched him and wondered what this big wop bastard wanted.

Carella wasn't about to tell him, not just yet he wasn't. Carella

56

wanted to know how come Corey hadn't mentioned anything about a crap game on his beat, especially since a man had been killed on Friday, and since the game had allegedly been running in the dead man's basement, under the dead man's aegis, for quite some time before he became a dead man. If Corey didn't know about the game, Carella wanted to know how come he didn't know about it? And if he did know about it, Carella wanted to know why it hadn't been mentioned? But in the meantime, he was willing to sit and smile at Corey and smoke a pleasant cigarette with the man, just the way the cops did it on television.

'What's up, Steve?' Corey asked.

'Well, I wanted your help on something,' Carella said.

Corey managed to suppress a sigh of relief and then smiled and took a deeper drag on his king-sized Chesterfield and said, 'Happy to help in any way I can, What's the problem?'

'A friend of mine is a little short of cash,' Carella said.

Corey, who had the cigarette in his mouth again and who was about to take another drag at it, stopped the action dead and quickly raised his eyes to meet Carella's across the desk. Being a crooked cop himself, he recognized Carella's gambit immediately. Carella's 'friend' who was a little short of cash was no one but Carella himself. And when a bull told you he was a little short of cash, he usually meant he wanted a cut of the pie or else he was going to start screaming to the captain about one violation or another.

'How short is your friend?' Corey asked, which meant *How much do you want in order to forget this whole matter?*

'Very very short,' Carella said gravely.

This was worse than Corey had expected. Carella seemed to be indicating that he wanted a bigger bite than any detective should normally expect. Detectives had their own little operations going and, like any good army, the officers didn't muscle in on the enlisted men's territory, and vice versa.

'Well, what did your friend have in mind?' Corey asked.

'I'd help him myself,' Carella said, 'but I'm not sure how.'

'I don't think I follow you,' Corey said, puzzled now.

'You're more in contact with things,' Carella said.

'What kind of things?' Corey asked.

'My friend craves action,' Carella said.

57

'What do you mean?' Corey said, and then squinted. 'Dames, you mean?'

'No.'

'I'm not with you, Steve.'

Corey was not being deliberately obtuse. He was simply having difficulty in adjusting his frame of reference. He had come up to the squadroom expecting God knew what kind of bullshit from Carella, and then had immediately realized that all Carella wanted was a percentage of the take. This hadn't surprised him at all, even though the word around the precinct was that Carella was a square cop who didn't take. Corey had met square cops who didn't take before. But what it turned out to be, after you knew these square cops for a while, was just that they were very quiet about taking, that was all. So Corey figured Carella wanted a piece of the action, which was all right with him so long as he got off his back, and so long as the tariff wasn't too steep. He'd begun to get nervous when Carella said he was *very* short of money, thinking this was going to be a real stickup. But then Carella seemed to switch in mid-stream and started talking about helping his friend *himself*, so that Corey figured maybe this really *was* a friend of Carella's. Then Carella had told him his friend craved action, and Corey had immediately begun thinking again that Carella's 'friend' was really Carella, just as he'd thought all along. What Carella wanted, Corey figured, was for Corey to fix him up quietly with one of the hookers on the beat, easy enough. But no, Carella said it wasn't dames.

'So what kind of action does your *friend* crave?' Corey asked, stressing the word 'friend' and making it clear he knew Carella's 'friend' was really Carella.

'Cards,' Carella said. 'Dice. Anything where he can parlay a small stake into some quick cash.'

'Oh,' Corey said. 'I see.'

'Mmm.'

'*Gambling* action, you mean.'

'Mmm.'

The men fell silent.

Corey drew in on his cigarette.

Carella waited.

'Gee, Steve,' Corey said at last, 'I wouldn't know *how* to help your friend.'

'You wouldn't, huh?'

'No, I'm sorry.'

'That's a shame,' Carella said.

'Yeah. But, you know, there's no gambling on my beat.'

'No.'

'No. Not to my knowledge, anyway,' Corey said, and smiled.

'Mmm,' Carella said.

'Yeah,' Corey said, and drew in on his cigarette again, and again the men were silent.

'That's too bad,' Carella said, 'because I had hoped maybe you'd know of a game.'

'No, I don't.'

'So I guess I'll have to scout one up on my own,' Carella said. He grinned. 'That can get expensive, of course, since I'd have to do it on my own time.'

'Yeah,' Corey said, 'I see what you mean.'

'Mmmm.'

'I could ... uh ... ask around, I guess. Maybe some of the boys know.'

'Well, I don't think the boys would know without *your* knowing, too, would they, Ralph?'

'Sometimes,' Corey said. 'You'd be surprised.'

'Yes, I would.'

'Huh?'

'I said I'd be surprised.'

'Well,' Corey said, rising, 'I'll ask around, Steve, and see what I can get for you.'

'Sit down a minute, Ralph,' Carella said. He smiled. 'Another cigarette?'

'No, No, thanks, I'm trying to cut down.'

'Ralph,' Carella said, 'would you like to tell me about the game in the basement of 4111 South Fifth?'

You had to hand it to Corey, Carella thought. His face did not change, he did not bat an eyelash, he simply sat opposite Carella and looked at him fiercely for several moments and then said, '4111?'

'Mmm.'

'South Fifth?'

'Mmm,' Carella said.

'Don't think I know the game you're referring to, Steve.'

Corey looked sincerely interested. 'Is it a card game?'

'Nope. Craps,' Carella said.

'I'll have to look into it. That's on my beat, you know.'

'Yes, I know. Sit down, Ralph, we're not finished yet.'

'I thought . . .'

'Yes, sit down.' Carella smiled again. 'Ralph, the man who was cutting the game wound up with an axe in his head. Name's George Lasser, the super of the building. Do you know him, Ralph?'

'Sure I do.'

'I think there may be a connection between the game and the murder, Ralph.'

'You do?'

'Yeah. That makes it a big-time game, doesn't it? That makes it a game involved in homicide.'

'I suppose it does. *If* there's a connection between the two.'

'Ralph, *if* there's a connection between the two, and *if* it turns out that somebody on the force deliberately withheld information about that game in the basement of 4111 where a man got murdered, that can be pretty serious, Ralph.'

'I suppose it can.'

'*Did* you know about the game, Ralph?'

'No.'

'Ralph?'

'Yeah?'

'We're going to find out.'

'Steve?'

'Yeah?'

'I've been a cop too long. Never shit a shitter, huh?' Corey smiled. 'The guy who was running the game is dead. If I was cutting that game, Steve, and I'm only saying *if* – if I was cutting that game, the only guy who'd know about it besides me would be the guy who was running the game, right? And he's dead, Steve. He got killed with an axe, Steve. So who are you trying to con?'

'I don't like you, Corey,' Carella said.

'I know that.'

'I haven't liked you from the minute I first saw you.'

'I know that, too.'

'If you're connected with this . . .'

'I'm not.'

'If you're connected with this, Corey, if you're making my job tougher, if you're hindering this case . . .'

'I don't know anything about your crap game,' Corey said.

'If you do, and if I find out that you do, I'm going to put your ass through the wringer, Corey. You're never going to look the same again.'

'Thanks for the warning,' Corey said.

'Now get the hell out of here.'

'Big detective,' Corey said, and he went out of the squadroom. He was smiling.

But he was worried.

The tenants of a building in a slum area do not much give a damn about whether or not cops solve the cases they are working on. As a matter of fact, if one were to take a poll of any tenement building at any given time of the year, one would probably discover that ninety-nine per cent of the tenants would like it if every cop in the world immediately dropped dead. Well, perhaps not in April. In April, the air is mild and the breezes are balmy, and brotherly love prevails, even towards cops. In April, it is possible that the tenants might only express the desire for every cop in the city to get hit by a bus – maimed, but not killed.

It was January.

Cotton Hawes had his hands full.

To begin with, the man would not let him into the basement.

He had never seen the man before. He was a giant of a man, perhaps sixty years old, with a European accent Hawes could not accurately place. He stood at the top of the steps leading to the basement and wanted to know just what the hell Hawes wanted, and there seemed to be about him a perfection of parts: the immense head with its thatch of unruly, sandy-coloured hair; the bulbous nose and large blue eyes and strong mouth and jaw; the thick neck and wide shoulders and chest, the muscular arms and huge hands – even the blue turtle-neck sweater under the brass-buttoned blue coveralls, all seemed of a piece, as though this man had been sculpted by someone with an excellent eye for proportion.

'I'm a police officer,' Hawes said. 'I want to have another look at that basement.'

'Let me see your badge,' the man said.

'Who are *you*?' Hawes asked.

'My name's John Iverson, I'm superintendent of the building next door, 4113.'

'Well, what are you doing *here*, if you're the super over *there*?'

'Mr Gottlieb, he's the landlord, he asked me if I could help out for a few days. Until he found somebody to take George's job.'

'Help out doing what?'

'Tend the furnace, get the garbage cans out in the morning. Same as I do next door.' Iverson paused. 'Let me see your badge '

Hawes showed Iverson his shield and then said, 'I'm going to be in the building most of the day, Mr Iverson, part of the time here in the basement and part of the time questioning the tenants.'

'Okay,' Iverson said, as though he were granting Hawes permission to remain. Hawes made no comment. Instead, he went down to the basement. Iverson followed him down the steps.

'Time to check the heat,' he said almost cheerfully and then went over to the black cast iron furnace sitting in one corner of the basement. He glanced at a gauge, picked up a shovel standing against the wall of the coal bin, and lifted open the furnace door with the blade of the shovel. He threw a dozen shovelfuls of coal into the furnace, slammed the door shut with the shovel, put the shovel back against the wall, and then leaned against the wall himself. Hawes stared at him across the length of the basement room.

'If you've got something else to do,' he said, 'don't let me hold you up.'

'I got nothing to do,' Iverson said.

'I thought maybe you wanted to go back next door and check the furnace there.'

'I done that before I come here,' Iverson said.

'I see. Well . . .' Hawes shrugged. 'What's this back here?' he asked.

'George's workbench.'

'What kind of work did he do?'

'Oh, odds and ends,' Iverson said.

Hawes studied the bench. A broken chair was on its top and alongside that a partially completed rung that would have replaced the broken one. There were three shelves hanging on the basement wall over the bench, all dust-covered, all crammed full of jars and tin cans containing nails, screws, and assorted hardware. Hawes looked at the shelves again. They were not, as he had first thought, *all* dust-covered. The middle one, in fact, had been wiped clean of dust.

'Anybody been down here since Friday?' he asked Iverson.

'No, I don't think so. They wouldn't let anyone come down. They were taking pictures, you know.'

'Who was?'

'The police.'

'I see,' Hawes said. 'Well, was anyone down here this morning?'

'Not from the police, no.'

'Anyone from the building?'

'Tenants come down here all the time,' Iverson said. 'There's a washing machine down here, same as in my building next door.'

'Where's that? The washing machine.'

'Over there. No, behind you.'

Hawes turned and saw the machine standing against one wall, its door open. He walked over towards it.

'Then anyone could have come down here this morning, is that right?' he asked. 'To use the machine?'

'That's right,' Iverson said.

'Did you see anyone come down?'

'Sure, I seen lots of tenants down here.'

'Which ones? Would you remember?'

'No.'

'Try.'

'I don't remember,' Iverson said.

Hawes grunted, barely audibly, and walked back to the workbench. 'Was Lasser working on this chair?' he asked.

'I don't know,' Iverson said. 'I guess so. If it's on his workbench, then I guess he was working on it.'

Hawes looked at the middle shelf again. It had definitely been wiped clean. He pulled his handkerchief from his back pocket, tented it over his hand, and pulled open one of the drawers under the workbench. The drawer was cluttered with old pencils, a straight edge, thumb tacks, a plumber's snake, a broken stapler, rubber bands, and a dusty package of Chiclets. Hawes closed the drawer. It went halfway into the bench, and then refused to move. He shoved at it again, cursed mildly, and then got on his hands and knees and crawled under the bench. He looked up at the drawer. The plumber's snake had caught on one of the cross supports, snagging the drawer. With one hand on the basement floor, close to the right rear leg of the bench, Hawes reached up and shoved at the snake, coiling it back into the drawer. He slid out from under the bench, dusted off his trousers, and closed the drawer.

'Is there a sink down here?' he asked.

'Over near the washing machine,' Iverson answered.

He walked away from the workbench and over to the sink against the opposite wall. A small covered drain was set into the basement floor in front of the sink. Hawes stopped with his feet on the drain cover, turned on the faucet, and began washing his hands with a bar of laundry soap that was resting in the basin.

'It gets dirty in basements,' Iverson said.

'Yeah,' Hawes answered.

He dried his hands on his handkerchief and then left the basement, walking directly out of the building, and to the corner, and into a candy store. From a pay-phone, he called the Police Laboratory and asked to talk to Detective-Lieutenant Sam Grossman.

'Hello?' Grossman said.

'Sam, this is Cotton Hawes. I'm here on South Fifth, just came from the basement. They tell me your boys were down there taking pictures.'

'Yeah, I suppose,' Grossman said.

'Sam, have you got any pictures of the dead man's workbench?'

'Which one is this, Cotton? Which case?'

'The axe murder. 4111 South Fifth.'

'Oh, yeah. Yeah. The workbench, huh? I think we've got some, why?'

'Have you looked them over yet?'

'Only casually. I just got to the office a little while ago. My brother got married last night.'

'Congratulations,' Hawes said.

'Thanks. What *about* the workbench?'

'Take another look at the pictures,' Hawes said. 'I don't know if it'll show or not, but there are three shelves over the bench. The middle shelf's been wiped clean of dust.'

'Yeah?'

'Yeah.'

'I'll take a look,' Grossman said. 'If it's anything, I'll follow it up.'

'Let us know, will you, Sam?'

'Who's working this with you?'

'Steve Carella.'

'Okay, I'll get back to you. Cotton?'

'I'm here.'

'This may take a while.'

'What do you mean?'

'I'll have to send a man down there, look over the place again, more pictures, maybe tests.'

'Okay, just let us know.'

'Right. Thanks a lot.'

Hawes hung up and walked back to Lasser's building. He wanted more than ever now to question the tenants in the building. Someone had wiped off that middle shelf, and he wondered who, and he wondered why.

It was unfortunate that he was a cop who looked like a cop. That's the worst kind of cop you can possibly be when you're questioning people who dislike cops as a matter of principle. Hawes was six feet two inches tall, and he weighed one hundred and ninety pounds. He had blue eyes and a square jaw with a cleft chin. His hair was red, except for a streak over his left temple where he had once been knifed and where the hair had curiously grown in white after the wound had healed. He had a straight unbroken nose, and a good mouth with a wide lower lip, but there was a look of arrogance on his face even when he was in a good mood. He was not in a good mood when he began questioning the tenants in the building, and he was in a worse mood after he had gone through two and a half floors of snotty answers and surly attitudes.

It was now twelve noon, and he was hungry, but he wanted to wrap up the third floor before he went to lunch, which would leave him three more floors to tackle in the afternoon. There were four apartments on each floor, and he had already questioned the tenants of 3A and 3B, which left 3C and 3D and then twelve more tenants on floors four to six inclusive, some way to spend a Monday. The word had flashed through the building the

65

moment he'd climbed the front stoop and entered the rank-smelling foyer, so everyone in the building knew that fuzz was on the scene, which wasn't very surprising anyway, considering the fact that old Georgie Lasser had had his head opened for him on Friday afternoon last week. Nobody liked fuzz, especially on Monday, especially in January, so Hawes had his work cut out for him.

He knocked on the door to 3C and, getting no answer, knocked again. He was about to move on to 3D when he heard a voice inside the apartment say, 'Georgie? Is that you?'

The voice was a young voice, and a weak one, and Hawes at first thought it belonged to someone who was sick, and then a couple of things occurred to him as he backed up to the door again. First, since everyone in the building knew John Law was here, why did that voice inside apartment 3C ask if he was Georgie? And second, Georgie *who*? The only Georgie that Hawes could think of at the moment was a dead man named George Lasser.

He knocked on the door again.

'Georgie?' the voice asked. The voice was still quiet, subdued; Hawes tried to remember where he had heard a similar voice before.

'Yes,' he answered. 'It's Georgie.'

'Just a minute,' the voice said.

He waited.

He heard footsteps approaching the door. Whoever did the walking was barefoot. He heard the rigid bar of a police lock being taken out of its plate screwed into the door, and then a chain being slipped out of its metal track, and then the door's regular lock being turned, the tumblers falling, the door opening a crack.

'You're not . . .' the voice said, but Hawes' foot was already in the door. Whoever was behind the door tried to slam it shut, but Hawes pushed his shoulder against it at just that moment and the door flew back and inward, and Hawes was inside the apartment.

The apartment was dark. The shades were drawn and there was the smell of urine and stale cigarette smoke and human perspiration and something else. The man standing before Hawes was in rumpled striped pyjamas. A five-day stubble covered

66

his face and he was badly in need of a haircut. His feet were dirty and there were yellow stains on his fingers and on his teeth. Through the open door behind him, Hawes could see a bedroom and a bed with twisted sheets. A girl was on the bed. She was wearing only a soiled slip, the nylon pulled high up over one scarred thigh.

If nothing else in the apartment spelled junkie, the girl's thigh did.

'Who the hell are *you*?' the man asked.

'Police,' Hawes said.

'Prove it.'

'Don't get smart, sonny boy,' Hawes said, pulling his wallet from his pocket. 'From the looks of this, you're in enough trouble already.'

'Maybe you're in trouble for unlawful entry,' the man said, looking at Hawes' shield held up in front of his face. Hawes put the wallet back into his trouser pocket and walked to the kitchen window. He raised the shade and opened the window and, over his shoulder, said, 'Have you given up breathing, or what?'

'What the hell do you want, cop?' the man asked.

'What's your name?'

'Bob Fontana.'

'And the girl?'

'Ask *her*,' Fontana said.

'I will, when she comes around. Meanwhile, suppose you tell me.'

'I forget,' Fontana said, and he shrugged.

'How long have you been holed up in here?'

'I don't know. What's today?'

'Monday.'

'Monday? Already?'

'You mind if I let some more air in here?'

'What are you? A fresh air fiend?'

Hawes went into the bedroom and opened the two windows there. The girl on the bed did not stir. As he rounded the bed, he pulled the slip down over the backs of her legs.

'What's the matter, cop?' Fontana asked. 'You don't like pussy?'

'How long has she been stoned like that?' Hawes asked.

'How do I know? I can't even remember her name.'

67

'Is she alive?' Hawes asked.

'I hope so. She's breathing, ain't she?'

Hawes lifted the girl's wrist and felt for her pulse. 'Barely,' he said. 'When did you shoot up?'

'I don't know what you mean by shoot up,' Fontana said.

Hawes picked up a charred tablespoon from the seat of a chair alongside the bed. 'What's this, Fontana?'

'It looks like a spoon to me. Maybe somebody was having some soup.'

'All right, where is it?'

'Where's what? The soup?'

'The junk, Fontana.'

'Oh, is that what you came in here for?'

'It's all gone, huh?' Hawes said.

'Well now, I don't know. You seem to be asking the questions and answering them all at the same time.'

'Okay,' Hawes said, 'let's take it from the top. How long have you been in this apartment?'

'Since New Year's Eve.'

'Celebrating, huh? And the girl?'

'The girl is my sister, don't bug me,' Fontana said.

'What's her name?'

'Louise.'

'Louise Fontana?'

'Yeah.'

'Where does she live?'

'Here, where do you think?'

'And you?'

'Here.' Fontana saw Hawes' look. 'Get your mind out of the gutter, cop. I sleep on the couch there.'

'How old is she?'

'Twenty-two.'

'And you?'

'Twenty-six.'

'How long have you been hooked?'

'I don't know what hooked means. You got something to pin on me, pin it. Otherwise, get the hell out.'

'Why? You expecting someone?'

'Yeah, I'm expecting President Johnson. He's coming here to

68

discuss the Russian situation. He comes here every Monday for lunch.'

'Who's Georgie?' Hawes said.

'I don't know. Who's Georgie?'

'When I knocked on the door, you asked if I was Georgie.'

'Did I?'

'Georgie who?'

'Georgie Jessel. He comes with the president every Monday.'

'Or maybe some other Georgie, huh?' Hawes said. 'You mind if I go through some of these drawers?'

'I think you'd better get a search warrant before you go messing up my underwear,' Fontana said.

'Well, that poses a slight dilemma,' Hawes said. 'Maybe you can help me with it.'

'Sure, glad to help the law anytime,' Fontana said, and rolled his eyes.

'There's no law against being an addict, you know that I guess.'

'I don't even know what an addict is.'

'But there *is* a law against possessing certain specified amounts of narcotics. Now here's the dilemma, Fontana. I can't pinch you unless I can prove possession. Well, I can't prove possession unless I make a search. And I can't make a search without a warrant. But if I go downtown for a warrant, by the time I come back you'll have flushed whatever I was looking for down the toilet. So what do I do?'

'Why don't you go home and sleep it off?' Fontana said.

'Of course, if I make an illegal search and come up with six pounds of uncut heroin . . .'

'Fat chance.'

'. . . why then nobody's going to worry about whether or not I had a warrant, are they?'

'Who's gonna worry, anyway? Who you trying to kid, cop? The last time I seen a cop with a search warrant in this neighbourhood, it was snowing inside the church in the middle of July. You're worried about a warrant, don't make me laugh. You bust down the door, and then suddenly you get legal? Ha!'

'Nobody broke down the door, Fontana.'

'No, you just give me the foot-and-shoulder treatment, that's all. Listen, I know cops. You're gonna search the pad, anyway, so what's the song and dance? Get it over with so I can get back to sleep.'

'You know what, Fontana?'

'What?'

'I think you're clean.'

'You know it, cop.'

'Otherwise, you wouldn't be so anxious for me to search.'

'Cool. So if you're done here, why don't you cut out, huh?'

'Why? Don't you want me to be here when Georgie arrives?'

'I told you, I'm sleepy, I want to get back to bed.'

'On the couch.'

'Yeah, on the couch,' Fontana said. 'She really *is* my sister, so quit bugging me.'

'What's her name?'

'Lois.'

'You said Louise last time around.'

'I said Lois.'

'Do you always refer to your sister as pussy?'

'It's what she is, ain't it? Being my sister don't make her better than anybody else. Girls are pussy, and that's all they are.'

'You're a sweet guy, Fontana. When did you have a bath last?'

'What are you? A cop or a department of sanitation? If you're finished, good-bye. I'm sick of this jazz.'

'Suppose I told you Georgie isn't coming today?'

'No?'

'No. Suppose I told you he isn't coming ever again?'

'Why not?'

'Guess.'

'That's the oldest trick in the book, cop. You want me to say, "Georgie ain't coming 'cause he got busted," and then you'll say, "Busted for what?" Only, I ain't biting, cop.'

'Try this one for size,' Hawes said.

'Yeah?'

'Georgie ain't coming 'cause he's dead.'

Fontana said nothing. He looked at Hawes silently and then wiped a hand over his mouth.

'Yeah,' Hawes said. 'Dead as a mackerel.'

'I'm from Missouri,' Fontana said.

'You've been in here since New Year's Eve,' Hawes said. 'That was last Tuesday. Georgie got it Friday.'

70

'When Friday?'

'In the afternoon. Sometime between one and two, near as we can make it.'

'Where?'

'Downstairs in the basement,' Hawes said.

'What the hell was Georgie doing in the basement?' Fontana asked.

Hawes stared at him.

'You didn't answer me,' Fontana said.

'Georgie Lasser?' Hawes said. 'Is that who we're . . .'

Fontana smiled.

'Wrong number, cop,' he answered.

Bob Fontana had been expecting a visit from someone named Georgie when Hawes knocked on the door. It was unfortunate that the Georgie he'd been expecting hadn't turned out to be the dead Georgie Lasser because that would have meant Lasser was involved with narcotics which could have explained a lot of things. Narcotics is very big time all over the world, bigger than prostitution and bigger than gambling, in fact probably the biggest of all underworld activities in terms of energy expended and capital realized. If a man is messing around with the dope business, anything can be anticipated – including an axe in the head. It was therefore unfortunate that Bob Fontana was not expecting Georgie Lasser, but some other Georgie instead. If Lasser had been a pusher, the cops might have had a new place to hang their hats. Instead, they were stuck with the same empty pegs.

Anyway, so it shouldn't be a total loss, Hawes decided to stick around until Georgie Whatever-His-Name-Was showed up. The day was half-shot anyway, so he figured he might as well make a narcotics pinch, thereby helping out the much overworked men in the city's Narcotic Division. The only trouble was that everyone in the building knew there was fuzz on the third floor, in Bobby the Junkie's apartment to be exact. Which might have explained why Georgie never showed up that afternoon.

Hawes hung around waiting for Georgie until almost three o'clock. He kept asking Fontana what Georgie's last name was, but Fontana kept telling him to go to hell. Hawes searched the apartment and, as he'd expected, found nothing but a lot of dirty

71

socks. At two-thirty, the girl woke up. Hawes asked her what her name was, and she said Betty O'Connor. He asked her how old she was, and she said twenty-two, which meant he couldn't even get Fontana on a morals charge. At two thirty-five, the girl asked Hawes if he had a cigarette, and Hawes gave her one and then she asked him if Georgie had arrived yet. Fontana quickly informed the girl that Hawes was a cop. The girl looked Hawes over, figured she was in some kind of trouble, not sure just *which* kind yet because she had just come back from a long journey over soft white hills on the backs of giant purple swans, but cops meant trouble and when you're in trouble you do what your mother taught you to do.

'Would you like to get laid?' she asked Hawes very sweetly.

It was the best offer he'd had all day, that was for sure. But he turned it down, anyway. Instead, he left the apartment, questioned the rest of the people in the building and got back to his own place at seven thirty-five that night.

He called Carella to tell him he had found two dusty shelves and a clean one.

six

Neither Carella nor Hawes so much as thought about the Lasser case until Friday of that week, when Danny Gimp called the office and asked Carella to meet him. Up to that time, they had been separately involved in handling a few other pressing matters that had come up.

There was, for example, a man in the precinct who kept making obscene phone calls to various and sundry ladies, explaining just what he would like to do to them, and apparently using language that even the boldest of the ladies refused to repeat to the police. In the short period of time between Tuesday and Friday mornings, Carella listened to the complaints of fourteen women who had been so abused on the telephone. At the same time, he answered twenty-two outside squeals, catching in

72

tandem with Hawes who answered twenty-seven. These complaints ranged from simple idiotic things like wife-beating (well, not so idiotic to the wife who was being clobbered, true, but annoying to a detective who had homicide to worry about) to burglary to unlawful assembly to stickups to prostitution (even though there was a Vice Squad) to auto thefts (even though there was an Automobile Squad) to a cat who had climbed a television antenna and refused to come down (the beat cop had tried to remove her and had his face and his right hand clawed) to several other pretty and not so pretty happenings.

One of the prettier happenings was a girl who had stripped down to her bra and panties in forty-degree January weather and gone for a swim in the Grover Park Lake. Since the lake fell well within the 87th Precinct territory, and since an ugly crowd had begun threatening the patrolman who tried to arrest the half-naked girl as she came out of the water, the precinct was called and a detective requested, so Carella got to see a pretty girl shivering in her underwear.

One of the not so pretty happenings was a January rumble between two street gangs, rare for January; most gangs save their rumbles for the good old summertime when tempers are hot and body odour is an additional secret weapon. A seventeen-year-old boy was left lying and bleeding beside a lamppost, trying to hold his intestines inside his body, embarrassed because all these people – including the teenage girl who had caused the rumble – were looking at him with his insides exposed. The interne had pulled a sheet over the boy, but his blood had stained through the sheet almost instantly and then a yellow pus-like slime had spread out onto the asphalt and Carella had wanted to puke. That was one of the not so pretty happenings.

Hawes had witnessed a man dying and had tried to get a dying statement from him, valid in court, but the man kept spitting blood onto his pillow because there were four ice-pick punctures in his chest, and then he sat up straight and stared at Hawes and said, 'Papa, Papa', and pulled Hawes close to him in a dying grip, spitting blood onto the shoulders of Hawes' sports jacket. Hawes washed the blood off in the kitchen of the small apartment and watched the lab boys dusting for prints.

An hour later he questioned a bewildered and frightened jeweller named Morris Seigel who had owned a store on Ainsley

Avenue for the past twenty years and who had been held up three times a year like clockwork for fifteen out of those twenty. This time the stickup man had come in at twelve-thirty in the afternoon and stuffed everything he could find into a big canvas bag he was carrying and then, not liking the way Seigel's head sat on his shoulders, had pistol whipped him so that Hawes now spoke to a man whose shattered eyeglasses hung askew on his bleeding face, the tears mingling with the blood on his cheeks.

He had gone out on a squeal involving a man who'd fallen onto the subway tracks at Seventeenth and Harris, he had answered a call from the owner of an ice-cream parlour who claimed that someone had ripped his pay telephone out of the booth and run off with it, he had answered three squeals for missing children and one from a man who shouted hysterically, 'My wife's in bed with another man! My wife's in bed with another man!'

It had been a busy few days.

On Friday morning, January 10th, Danny Gimp called and asked to talk to Steve Carella, who was on his way out to investigate, in order, a call from a literary agency where two typewriters had been stolen, a call from a woman who complained of a peeping Tom, and a call from a supermarket manager who believed someone was dipping into the till.

'I think I may have something,' Danny said.

'Can you meet me right now?' Carella asked.

'I'm still in bed.'

'When then?'

'This afternoon.'

'What time?'

'Four,' Danny said, 'the corner of Fiftieth and Warren.'

At 9.27 a.m., Carella left the squadroom to begin answering his squeals, hoping he'd be finished by four in the afternoon. He said good-bye to Hawes who had decided to visit the Lasser family doctor in New Essex and who was on the phone at the moment arguing with Dave Murchison downstairs about the use of a police sedan.

'Hey,' Carella said. 'I said good-bye.'

'Okay, I'll see you later.'

'Let's hope Danny comes up with something.'

'Let's hope,' Hawes said, and he waved at Carella as he walked

74

through the gate in the railing, and then he turned his attention back to the phone and began yelling at Murchison again. Murchison wasn't buying any, thanks. Hawes told him his own car was in the garage with alignment trouble, but Murchison steadfastly maintained that each of the precinct's sedans was either in use or about to be used that morning, and he couldn't let Hawes have one even if Hawes brought in the commissioner personally, or perhaps even the mayor. Hawes told him to go to hell. As he was leaving the precinct on the way to the train station, he pointedly walked past the muster desk without saying a word to Murchison. Murchison, busy with the switchboard, didn't even notice Hawes going by.

Dr Ferdinand Matthewson was an old man with a leonine mane of white hair, a long nose and a gentle voice that issued sibilantly from between pursed lips. He wore a dark black suit and he kept his hands, brown with liver spots, tented in front of his face as he sat in a big brown leather chair and watched Hawes intently and suspiciously.

'How long has Mrs Lasser been ill?' Hawes asked.

'Since 1939,' Matthewson said.

'When in 1939?'

'September.'

'How would you describe her present condition?'

'Paranoid schizophrenia.'

'Do you feel Mrs Lasser should be institutionalized, sir?'

'Definitely not,' Matthewson said.

'Even though she has been schizophrenic since 1939?'

'She is dangerous neither to herself nor society. There is no reason for her to be institutionalized.'

'Has she ever *been* institutionalized?'

Matthewson hesitated.

'Doctor?'

'Yes, I heard you.'

'Has she ever been institutionalized?'

'Yes.'

'When?'

'In 1939.'

'For how long?'

Again, Matthewson hesitated.

75

'For how long, sir?'

'Three years.'

'Where?'

'I don't know.'

'You're her family physician, aren't you?'

'I am.'

'Then where was she institutionalized? Can you tell me that?'

'I want no part of this, sir,' Matthewson said suddenly. 'I want no part of what you're trying to do.'

'I'm trying to investigate a murder,' Hawes said.

'No, sir. You are trying to send an old woman back into an institution, and I will not help you to do that. No, sir. There has been too much misery in the lives of the Lassers. I will not help you to add to it. No, sir.'

'Dr Matthewson, I assure you I am . . .'

'Why must you do this?' Matthewson asked. 'Why won't you let a sick old woman live out her days in peace, cared for and protected by someone who loves her?'

'I'm sorry, Dr Matthewson. I'd like to let *everybody* live out his days in peace. But somebody just wouldn't allow George Lasser to do that.'

'Estelle Lasser didn't kill her husband, if that's what you think.'

'No one said she did.'

'Then why do you want to know about her condition? She's been hopelessly out of her mind since September of 1939 when Tony left for . . .' Matthewson clamped his mouth shut. 'Never mind,' he said. 'I wish you'd get out of here, sir. I wish you would leave me alone.'

Hawes continued to sit calmly on the other side of Matthewson's desk. Calmly, he said, 'Dr Matthewson, we are investigating a murder.'

'I don't care what you . . .'

'We can bring charges against you for impeding the progress of an investigation, but I would prefer not to do that, sir. I'll tell you simply that it is entirely within the realm of possibility for Mrs Lasser to have killed her own husband. It is also within that realm of possibility for Anthony Lasser to have . . .'

'Both of those suppositions are *entirely* absurd,' Matthewson said.

'If they're so damn absurd, sir, maybe you'd like to tell me just why.'

'Because Estelle hasn't known her husband or anyone else since that September in 1939. And Tony Lasser hasn't stepped out of that house on Westerfield Street since he returned home from Virginia in June of 1942. That's why. You are dealing with a delicately constructed symbiosis here, Mr Hawes, and if you tamper with it, you are liable to destroy two people who have known enough misery in their lives.'

'Tell me about it,' Hawes said.

'I have told you all I care to tell you. I will contribute nothing further to your cause. I ask you in all humility to please, please leave these people alone. They could not possibly have had anything to do with the murder of George Lasser. If you lift this rock, Mr Hawes, you will find only blind, albino creatures scurrying helplessly from the sun. I beg you not to do that.'

'Thank you, Dr Matthewson,' Hawes said.

He rose and left the office.

Hawes was not a firm believer in old adages, but there was an old adage that ran to the tune of Where There's Smoke There's Fire, and there sure as hell seemed to be a lot of smoke gushing up from Estelle Lasser and her son Tony. The first thing that occurred to Hawes was the possibility that someone had lodged a complaint against Estelle before she'd been institutionalized in 1939, so he ambled over to the New Essex Police station, introduced himself, and asked to see their records for that year. The New Essex Police, always anxious to co-operate with big city detectives – ha – ! – happily opened their files to him, and Hawes spent a slow hour and a half perusing the misdemeanours and felonies that had plagued that fair hamlet back in the good old days. Unfortunately, Mrs Lasser had committed neither felony nor misdemeanour; nowhere in the records was there listed any official complaint against her. Hawes thanked the police, and walked over to the New Essex Hospital where he similarly requested a look at their voluminous medical files.

An ambulance call *had* been made to the home of Mr George Lasser, 1529 Westerfield Street, on the night of September 11, 1939. Mrs Lasser had been admitted to the hospital at 8.27 p.m. for observation and had been transferred to Buena Vista, in the

77

city, for further tests on September 13, 1939. Hawes thanked the clerk in the records room, and then walked to the railroad station. He had a quick hot dog and orange drink at a stand there, and then caught the 12.14 back to the city. He changed his seat three times, moving to a different car each time because it seemed someone on the railroad had decided to turn up the air-conditioning. This was perfectly reasonable since the system probably hadn't been functioning properly during July and August and, it now being January, what better time to check it? But Hawes nonetheless changed his seat three times, seeking warmth, and finally found a facsimile of it by concentrating on the crossed legs of a redhead for the remainder of the trip.

The psychiatrist he spoke to at Buena Vista was a youngish man who had been at the hospital for no more than five years and who did not remember Estelle Lasser. He was reluctant to open the hospital files without either a court order or a release from the patient, but Hawes explained that he was seeking information which might be pertinent in a murder case, and that he was certain he could obtain the necessary court order simply by making the necessary trip downtown. The psychiatrist was still reluctant to dig out Estelle Lasser's records because he was fully aware that she could sue him for divulging this information to the police, but Hawes assured the psychiatrist that Mrs Lasser was still ill and hardly in condition to go suing anyone. With a great deal of muttering and head-shaking, the psychiatrist went to the files and informed Hawes that Mrs Lasser had indeed undergone a series of psychiatric tests during the month of September in 1939. The doctor looked up at this point and mused that Hitler was invading Poland at about that same time. Hawes nodded and agreed that it sure was a small world.

'Can you tell me the facts of the case?' he asked.

'Yes, certainly. On September 11, 1939, about a week after her young son had been sent off to school, Mrs Lasser . . .'

'What school was that? Does it say?'

'Yes. Soames Academy. In Richmond, Virginia.'

'That's a private school, isn't it?'

'Yes.'

'Go on,' Hawes said.

'Well, Mrs Lasser tried to kill herself, that's all,' the psychiatrist said.

78

'I see.'

'It turned out that this was the third time she'd attempted suicide since her son had left for school at the beginning of September. This time, her husband really became alarmed and called for an ambulance. She was taken to the hospital in New Essex. They made the preliminary examination and then suggested that we conclude the tests. We have a greater psychiatric facility here, you see.'

'I see. And what was the diagnosis, doctor?'

'She was a schizophrenic of the paranoid type,' the doctor said.

'And the disposition of the case?'

'We told Mr Lasser that his wife needed extensive hospitalization and therapy, and asked that he commit her to an institution. He refused, apparently upon the advice of his family physician. We asked for a legal commitment.'

'What's the difference?' Hawes asked.

'Well, if a person is legally committed, it means that she cannot be returned to society until the director of the hospital recommends her release.'

'And would her case then go before the court?'

'Not unless there were criminal charges pending. I don't believe there were any here.' He consulted his records. 'No, there were none. Her release, then, would have been left entirely to the discretion of the hospital director.'

'Where was Mrs Lasser sent? To a state hospital?'

'No, sir. Mr Lasser requested that she be sent to a private institution. The request was granted by the court.'

'The court? I thought you just said . . .'

'Yes, Mr Hawes, the court. There were no criminal charges, you understand, but a legal commitment *must* be requested in a court. In this state, a superior court. And two qualified psychiatrists must sign the commitment papers.'

'Aren't private institutions expensive?' Hawes asked.

'What?'

'Private institutions. Are they . . .?'

'Well, yes, they are.'

'How much do they cost?'

'Well, a good one will charge somewhere between two and three hundred dollars a week.'

'And was Mrs Lasser sent to a good one?'

'Yes, sir. She was sent to the Mercer Sanitarium, right here in the city. It has an excellent reputation.'

'I see,' Hawes said. 'Thank you very much, doctor. You've been most helpful.'

The Mercer Sanitarium was on a tree-lined sidestreet in Riverhead, at the other end of the city. Hawes had gone from the squadroom to New Essex, which was about fifteen miles East of Riverhead, and then to the Buena Vista Hospital, which was about fifteen miles West of Riverhead, and then back uptown again to the tree-lined sidestreet upon which sat the huge white Georgian Colonial surrounded by a simple black wrought iron fence. There was no sign outside the sanitarium, nor were there any white-frocked attendants or nurses in evidence. The fence around the place was low enough for a child to have leaped. There were no bars or wire mesh on any of the windows fronting the street. In short, there was no indication – save for the fact that it was the only building on the block – that this was a place for the mentally ill.

Hawes announced himself to a receptionist wearing a white nurse's uniform, telling her he was a detective, and showing her his shield and his I.D. card. The receptionist seemed singularly unimpressed. She asked Hawes to please be seated, and then she opened a huge mahogany door and was gone for several moments. When she returned, she asked Hawes if he would mind waiting just a short while, and Hawes said he wouldn't mind waiting, and then glanced at his watch. This was Friday, the beginning of the weekend, and he had a dinner date with Christine.

At the end of what seemed like a half-hour but what was actually ten minutes, the mahogany door opened and a very good-looking woman in a tailored blue suit, perhaps forty-five years old, her brown hair pulled to the back of her head in a severe bun, a pleasant welcoming smile on her face, stepped into the small entrance alcove and said, 'Detective Hawes?'

Hawes rose from where he was sitting on the bench. 'Yes,' he said, and extended his hand. 'How do you do?'

'How do you do?' the woman said, taking his hand. 'I'm Mrs Mercer. Won't you please come in?'

He followed Mrs Mercer through the doorway and into an office panelled with the same rich mahogany as the door. She gestured to a paisley wingchair in front of a very large desk, the top of which was covered with a sheet of glass perhaps a half-inch thick. The desk was piled high with what Hawes assumed were case histories in worn blue binders. A framed diploma on the wall behind the desk advised Hawes that someone named Geraldine Porter (he figured this was Mrs Mercer's maiden name) had been graduated from Boston University with a Bachelor of Science degree. A second framed document told him that Geraldine Porter Mercer (he'd been right about the maiden name) had completed the course of study for a Master's Degree in Psychology at Cornell University. There were other framed documents on the wall, all of which were awards or commendations of one kind or another from groups as disparate as the A.M.A. and Hadassah, some acknowledging the high standards and service to the medical community of the Mercer Sanitarium, and others honouring Mrs Mercer personally.

'Yes, Detective Hawes, what can I do for you?' she asked. There was a broad A in her speech, partially obscured by years of living here in Riverhead. Hawes smiled in recognition, and she smiled back at him and said, 'Yes?'

'Boston,' he answered simply.

'Close,' she said. 'West Newton.'

'The same thing.'

'Possibly,' Mrs Mercer said, and smiled again. 'You still haven't told me why you're here.'

'A man named George Lasser was killed yesterday afternoon,' Hawes said. He watched her face. Not a trace of recognition flickered in the blue eyes. The full mouth remained placid. There was in her manner only an attitude of polite expectancy. She said nothing. 'His wife's name was Estelle Valentine Lasser,' Hawes said.

'Oh,' Mrs Mercer said. 'Yes.'

'Does the name mean anything to you?'

'Yes. She was a patient here.'

'That's right.'

'Yes, I remember. This was quite some time ago, Mr Hawes.' She smiled and said, 'Do I call you Mr Hawes or Detective Hawes, which? It's a little puzzling.'

'Whichever you prefer,' Hawes said, smiling back.

'Mr Hawes then,' she said. 'Oh, I would say Mrs Lasser was

81

with us in the very early days of the sanitarium. My husband opened the hospital in 1935, you see, and this must have been shortly after that.'

'Mrs Lasser was committed in 1939,' Hawes said.

'Yes, that's right.'

'Can you tell me about it?'

'Well, what would you like to know?'

'How much did she pay?'

'What?'

'This is a private hospital,' Hawes said. 'How much was Mrs Lasser paying for her care in 1939?'

'Well, I wouldn't know exactly. I would have to check our records. As a matter of fact, I doubt if they'd go back that far.'

'Your financial records, do you mean?'

'Yes. Our medical records go back to the beginning, of course.'

'Well, can you make a *guess* at what your charges were in 1939? Approximately?'

'I would say a hundred dollars a week. Or perhaps a hundred and a quarter. Certainly no more than that.'

'And Mr Lasser agreed to pay these charges?'

'I assume so. His wife *was* a patient here, so I assume . . .'

'Did he ever miss any payments?'

'I really don't know. Mr Hawes, if this is important, I'll see if we have the records. But I . . .'

'We can check it later,' Hawes said. 'Can you tell me how long Mrs Lasser was a patient here?'

'She was released in June of 1942 on the recommendation of my husband.'

'And was your husband convinced at that time that Mrs Lasser was legally sane?'

'Legally sane is a meaningless phrase,' Mrs Mercer said. 'It has been forced upon the medical profession by our courts. If you mean did my husband believe Mrs Lasser was ready to return to her family, yes my husband believed so. If you mean did he believe Mrs Lasser would no longer attempt to harm herself or anyone else, yes my husband believed so. Moreover, this was an opportune time for her to return home. Her illness started when her son left for school, you know. Or at least, that was when it first made itself manifest. Well, her son was eighteen and returning home from school that June. My husband's timing was very carefully calculated. Naturally, he had no way of foreseeing what would happen to Tony.'

'What *did* happen, Mrs Mercer?'

'Well . . . have you met him?'

'Yes.'

'He has developed a phobic reaction to the outdoors,' Mrs Mercer said.

'Which means?'

'Which means he will not leave the house.'

'*Will* not, or *cannot*?'

'Cannot, if you prefer.'

'I'm asking, Mrs Mercer. Is his leaving the house a matter of choice? Or would it be *impossible* for him to leave it?'

'From what I understand, Mr Hawes, and I assure you we have not done a follow-up on Mrs Lasser since – oh, 1945 – from what I understand, Tony Lasser has not left that house in New Essex since he returned from prep school in June of 1942. That is a long long time, Mr Hawes. Are you familiar with the nature of phobic reactions?'

'No, not exactly.'

'A phobia is really . . . well, how can I put it? . . . a *binding* of anxiety. Once the anxiety is bound . . .'

'What's anxiety?' Hawes asked.

'Ah, a twentieth century man who doesn't know the meaning of anxiety,' Mrs Mercer said, and smiled.

'Is that bad?'

'If you've never experienced it, it's good,' she answered. 'Anxiety is a state of apprehension or psychic tension found in most forms of mental disorders. In Tony Lasser's case, he has chosen to deal with his anxiety by accepting the symptoms of a phobia instead.'

'But why won't he leave the house?' Hawes asked.

'Because it would be extremely painful for him if he did.'

'In what way?'

'He might begin trembling or sweating, he might suffer palpitations, he might feel faint or might actually faint, he might experience a sinking sensation in his stomach . . .' Mrs Mercer shrugged. 'In other words, extreme anxiety.'

'But in spite of all this, could he leave the house if he wanted to?'

'Well . . .'

'I mean, if the house were on fire, for example, he probably would try to get out, isn't that so?'

'Probably, yes. Depending upon how strong his phobia is. Generally speaking, I suppose we could say that the real fear of fire, the immediate presence of fire, might be stronger than any phobic reaction in such a person.'

'Then Lasser *could* have left the house?' Hawes said. 'He *could* have murdered his father?'

'Well, I don't know,' Mrs Mercer said, and shrugged. 'Possibly. There would have been a great deal of anxiety involved, of course. But possibly he might have risked that if the urge to kill were strong enough.'

'Thank you, Mrs Mercer.'

'I think it's *possible* he left the house, Mr Hawes. I do not, however, think it's very probable. Tony Lasser is not a patient of ours, so I don't really know very much about the origins and meaning of his phobia. But I *do* know that the last time he left that house, in 1939, his mother tried to kill herself. It is not very probable that he would try it again.'

'You mean he's afraid she might try suicide again?'

'Oh, that's much too surface, Mr Hawes. If the answer were that simple, I doubt very much there'd be a phobic reaction at all. I would rather suggest that perhaps he would *like* her to try suicide again.'

'What do you mean?'

'Perhaps he *wants* his mother dead. But he knows that if he leaves the house, she may attempt suicide again. This would grant his secret wish, and the prospect of such a wish coming true is so frightening, and brings on such anxiety, that he develops a phobia instead.'

'It sounds very complicated,' Hawes said, and sighed.

'Human beings *are* very complicated, Mr Hawes. Even well-adjusted ones.'

'I suppose so,' Hawes said, and smiled. He rose and extended his hand. 'Thank you very much for your time, Mrs Mercer. I know you're busy.'

'But must you go?' she asked. 'My husband is at a staff meeting right now, but he should be down shortly. We generally have tea at four.' She smiled. 'An old Boston custom, you know.'

'Yes, I heard about the party you had there,' Hawes answered.

84

'Won't you stay?'

'I was *raised* drinking tea, Mrs Mercer,' Hawes said.

'Then join us. I feel terribly guilty somehow. I feel I gave you information that doesn't help you at all.'

'Well, maybe my partner's doing a little better,' Hawes said. 'In any case, I would be delighted to have some tea with you and your husband.'

Danny Gimp, it seemed, was developing a taste for the great outdoors.

Carella didn't mind spending time in the fresh air, but he wished that Danny had exercised a bit more judgement in his choice of a location.

'Fiftieth and Warren,' Danny had said, undoubtedly picking this particular corner because it was several miles distant from the precinct. He could not have known. or perhaps he *did* know and was simply being ornery, that the right angle described by those cross streets neatly embraced an empty lot over which all the winds of January howled and screeched and ranted. Carella, his coat collar pulled high up on the back of his neck, his head tucked in like a turtle's, his ears numb, his coat flapping around his legs, his hands in his pockets, cursed Danny Gimp, and wondered why his father had ever left Italy. In Italy, when the *carabinieri* met a stool pigeon, it was probably at a sidewalk table in the sunshine. '*Buon giorno, tenente,*' the stoolie would say. '*Vuole un piccolo bicchiere di vino?*'

'Hello, Steve,' the voice behind him whispered.

He recognized the voice as Danny's, and turned immediately. Danny was wearing a heavy overcoat, a thick Irish tweed with an enormous collar that covered the back of his head. In addition, he was wearing a woollen muffler, and a checked cap, and bright yellow earmuffs. He looked cheerful and well-rested and warm as toast.

'Let's get the hell out of this cold,' Carella said. 'What is it with you, Danny? I remember times we used to meet like civilized people, in restaurants, in bars, what is it with this frozen tundra routine?'

'You cold?' Danny asked, surprised.

'I've been standing on this corner for the past fifteen minutes. Listen to that wind. It's from *Nanook of the North*.'

85

'Gee, I'm nice and warm,' Danny said.

'There's a cafeteria up the street. Let's try it,' Carella said. As they began walking, he asked, 'What'd you get for me?'

'Well, I found out about the game. I don't know what good it'll do you, but I found out about it.'

'Shoot.'

'First of all, it ain't regular, like you said it was. It's a some-time thing, whenever the urge strikes. Sometimes two, three times a week, and other times maybe only once a month, you dig?'

'I dig,' Carella said. 'In here.'

He pushed his way through the cafeteria's revolving door, and Danny followed him.

'I've always been afraid of revolving doors,' Danny said.

'How come?'

'I got caught in one when I was a kid.'

'You want some coffee?'

'Yeah, sure.'

They went to the counter, got two cups of coffee, and then found an empty table at the back of the place. Before they sat, Danny looked the place over very carefully. 'Lots of these all-night cafeterias are meeting places for junkies,' he said. 'I wanted to make sure nobody made us.'

'Okay,' Carella said, 'about the game.'

'I told you already that you were wrong about it being a regular thing, right?'

'Right. Go on.'

'Second, you were right about it being stationary. But, Steve, it's a very small game.'

'Are you talking about the number of players, or the bets?'

'Both. If they have ten guys playing each time, they're lucky.'

'That's a fairly big game,' Carella said.

'Nah, not really. I've seen blankets with two dozen guys around them.'

'Okay, what about the bets?'

'Smalltime stuff. There's no limit, but the bets hardly ever go higher than a buck or two, maybe on occasion a finnif. But that's it.'

'What about Lasser? Was he taking a house vigourish?'

'Nope.'

'What do you mean? He wasn't taking a cut?'

'Nope.'

'Then why'd he risk having the game in his basement?'

'I don't know, Steve.'

'This doesn't make much sense.'

'Neither do the players.'

'Who played, Danny?'

'Different guys each time, mostly very cheap hoods. Only two regulars, far as I can make out.'

'And who are they?'

'One is a guy named Allie the Shark Spedino, you know him?'

'Fill me in.'

'Very nothing,' Danny said. 'I think he served a few terms up at Castleview, I don't know for what.'

'Okay, who was the other regular?'

'Guy named Siggie Reuhr. Ever hear of him?'

'No.'

'Me neither. In any case, this game was strictly kindergarten stuff. There was no money in it, and the guys in it are practically anonymous, who the hell ever heard of them?'

'Did you find out whether there'd been any big winners?'

'How you gonna have big winners when you ain't got big money? Besides, if Lasser wasn't cutting the game, then why would anybody hold a grudge against him, big winner, big loser, or whatever?'

'Yeah, you're right. I don't get this, Danny.'

'Well, one thing's for sure,' Danny said. 'Whatever reason Lasser had for letting them use that basement, it wasn't 'cause he was taking any money out of the game.'

'Was he putting any *into* it?'

'What do you mean?'

'Did he play?' Carella asked.

'Nope. Sometimes he watched. Most of the time, he was off in another part of the basement, reading a paper or playing Solitaire, like that.'

'Who gave you this, Danny?'

'A guy who played in a few of the games before he realized they were gonna stay small potatoes.'

Carella shook his head. 'I don't get this. I really don't.'

'What don't you get?'

'Lasser was supposed to be making *money* out of these games. Anyway, that's what his friends told me.'

Danny shrugged. 'Friends don't always know,' he said. 'I'm telling you for sure, Steve. This was a nothing game. Lasser wasn't taking a penny out of it.'

'Maybe he was getting a flat rate from somebody. Couple of hundred every time they played, how about that?'

'Steve, this is a *nothing* game, you dig? A buck, two bucks at a time, that's all. So who's gonna give Lasser a couple of bills for running the game, would you mind telling me? There ain't that much money in the game itself!'

'Okay, maybe he got twenty-five bucks or so.'

'That's more sensible, but even that's high.'

'I don't think he'd risk it for less,' Carella said.

'What risk? Look, Steve, from what I got this game is common knowledge to every cop on the beat. Which means they're getting theirs, right? So what's the risk to Lasser? No risk at all. He lets them use the basement and he comes out of it smelling of roses, right?'

'He's just doing it as a favour, huh?' Carella asked.

'Why not? He's giving some guys a place to have a game. What's so hard to believe about that?'

'Nothing,' Carella said. 'I believe it.'

'So then what's the problem?'

'I'd like to know how Georgie Lasser, who lives on a nice respectable street in New Essex, comes to know a bunch of hoods who want to shoot dice in his basement.'

Danny shrugged. 'Why don't you ask the hoods?' he suggested.

'That's just what I plan to do,' Carella said.

seven

Allie the Shark Spedino came into the squadroom of his own volition at ten a.m. on the morning of Monday, January 13th. He had been out of the city all weekend, he explained, and he returned to discover from some of the neighbourhood guys that two bu ... two detectives from the eight-seven were looking for him. So, having nothing to hide, he figured he might as well come up to see them before they put out an all-points bulletin, ha ha ha.

Carella and Hawes let Spedino chuckle a bit and then asked him to take a seat. Spedino was not called Allie the Shark for nothing. He had a head and face that came to a sloping point at the front, like the nose of a shark, and he had small sharp little teeth that scared hell out of you whenever he smiled. In addition to that, he moved with a dancer's agility and grace so that he seemed to be gliding effortlessly through Caribbean waters hunting for skin-divers off coral reefs. He also gave an impression not of fearlessness but of plain unpredictability. You never knew whether splashing water in his face would send him swimming away in panic or would provoke him to a blood-thirsty attack. Carella hadn't liked him after reading his B-sheet, and he liked him even less in person, sitting opposite him at a squadroom desk.

They had requested a copy of Spedino's police record from the Bureau of Criminal Identification, Danny having told Carella that Spedino had served time up at Castleview on at least two separate occasions. The B.C.I. had promptly provided Carella with the information he'd asked for, and he and Hawes had gone over it in the squadroom on Saturday afternoon.

Now, in the warm comfort of the squadroom on Monday morning, Spedino grinned and asked, 'So why'd you want to see me?'

'Have you ever done time, Spedino?' Carella asked testing him.

'If you guys were looking for me, then you've already seen my B-sheet, and you know exactly what I done or I didn't do, right?' Spedino asked, and he smiled his small pointed shark smile.

'Well, let's assume we haven't seen your B-sheet and don't know a thing about you. Fill us in.'

'I took two falls,' Spedino said, the smile vanishing from his face to leave only a very serious circling shark look. 'I hung some paper back in 1930, and done five at Castleview, no parole.'

'First offence?' Carella asked.

'Yeah.'

'And you served the full term?'

'Yeah, well, I was eighteen at the time, you know, and I thought I was hot stuff. I didn't deserve to be paroled, believe me.'

'So you were released in 1935, is that right?'

'Yeah. And I was back in again in 1936, though not at Castleview.'

'Where, and what for?'

'I done six months on Walker Island for coercion.'

'Who'd you coerce?'

'I tried to convince this guy who worked for a bank to print up some cheques for me, with my name on them, you know?'

'How'd you try to convince him?'

'I told him I'd cut him up if he didn't get the cheques for me.'

'What happened?'

Spedino shrugged. 'He went to the cops. So I never got my cheques, and instead I got six months on Walker.'

'And since that time?' Hawes asked.

'Clean as a whistle.'

'Except for the crap games in Lasser's basements, huh?'

Spedino's expression did not change an iota. 'What crap games?' he asked. 'Who's Lasser?'

'George Lasser.'

'Never heard of him.'

'4111 South Fifth.'

'Where's that?'

'We know you were there, Spedino.'

'When was the game?' Spedino asked.

'Why? Are you going to tell us all about it?'

'No, I was trying to think how maybe I could have been mistaken for somebody else or something. That's why I wanted to know when the game was.'

'Spedino,' Carella said slowly, 'you're full of crap.'

'Well, that may be so,' Spedino said, smiling his shark grin, 'but the truth of the matter is that I have been clean since 1936 when I got off of Walker Island, and I never hope to see the inside of another prison again.'

'What you mean is that you hope you never get *caught* again, isn't that it, Spedino?'

'No, sir, I mean I have been on the straight and narrow since that time, that's what I mean.'

'Since 1936, is that right?'

'Yes, sir, since November of 1936, that is correct.'

90

'When did you meet Lasser? Around that time?'

'I do not know who Lasser is,' Spedino said. His speech, like his manner, had changed abruptly the moment the crap games had been mentioned. He tried very much to sound like an elocution professor now, which meant that he succeeded only in sounding like a cheap hood who had been convicted once for passing bum cheques and again for threatening someone with violence if he did not help Spedino in the pursuit of his chosen profession, which seemed to be the hanging of paper. At the same time, he sat up straight in the hard backed chair and tried to appear very dignified, which meant that he succeeded in looking like a shark who had somehow come to the surface in a dark blue suit and a grey tie and a neat grey fedora which was perched on his lap.

'Lasser is the man who allowed you to have your crap games in his basement,' Carella said. 'You and your friend Siggie Reuhr, who is the only other regular in the game. Who is he, Spedino? We don't have a record for him.'

'I never heard of him in my life,' Spedino said.

'Spedino, are you listening?' Carella asked.

'I'm listening.'

'Spedino, this is a homicide rap we're dealing with here.'

'What do you mean, a homicide rap?'

'This isn't a gambling misdemeanour or some more bum cheques being passed. This is a man dead with an axe in his head.'

'I wouldn't even touch a fly,' Spedino said, 'unless it was unzipped,' making a joke the detectives had heard a thousand times before. They continued to stare at him without smiling. 'Unless it was unzipped,' Spedino said again, as though repetition would improve the flavour, but the detectives still watched him unsmilingly.

'Homicide,' Hawes said.

'Homicide,' Carella repeated.

'Homicide, my ass,' Spedino answered angrily. 'What kind of phony rap you trying to hang on me? I never even heard of George Lasser, nor of this Sigmund Freud, either.'

'Siggie *Reuhr*,' Carella corrected.

'Yeah, him. What the hell is it with you guys, anyway? You can't bear to see somebody make good? I took two lousy falls back in the thirties, and you're still bugging me about them. Well, get off my back, huh? You got something to book me for? If not, either let me go, or let me call my lawyer.'

'Oh boy, we've got a real bigtime gangster in here,' Hawes said. 'Look at him, he's going to call his lawyer. Come on, we'll do a real Grade-B movie bit, okay, Spedino? You call your lawyer, and when he gets here we'll make like cops and call him "Counsellor" and everything, how's that?'

'Ha, ha, very funny,' Spedino said.

'Tell us about those crap games,' Carella said.

'I don't know any crap games. I don't even know how to shoot dice, that's the truth. Sevens, elevens, they're all the same to me.'

'Sure,' Carella said.

'Sure.'

'We would like to know what your connection with George Lasser is, or rather *was*,' Carella said. 'Now how about telling us what we want to know, Spedino, before we find something to hang around your neck.'

'What're you going to find, huh? Who you trying to kid? I'm clean as a whistle.'

'How have you been earning a living, Spedino?'

'I work in a book shop.'

'In a *what*?'

'It's impossible, huh? Impossible for a con to work in a book shop. Well, that's where I work.'

'Where? What book shop?'

'It's called The Bookends, and it's on Hampton Avenue, in Riverhead.'

'What's your boss' name?'

'Matthew Hicks.'

'How much does he pay you?'

'A hundred and seventeen dollars a week, that's after taxes.'

'And you try to lose it all in crap games, huh?'

'I don't try to lose it noplace,' Spedino said. 'I'm a married man with two kids, and I've been straight since 1936. Listen, I'm not a spring chicken any more, you know. I'm fifty-two years old.'

'George Lasser was eighty-seven,' Hawes said.

'That's a nice age,' Spedino answered, 'but I still don't know him.'

92

'We've just been misinformed, huh?' Carella said.

'I guess so.'

'You've never been anywhere near 4111 South Fifth and you never knew about a crap game going on down there in the basement, and you don't know George Lasser, nor Siggie Reuhr, either.'

'That's right,' Spedino said, nodding. 'You've got it all right.'

'We'll get back to you, Spedino,' Carella said.

'Can I go now?'

'Where were you this weekend?'

'Away, I told you.'

'Where?'

'I took the family to Jersey for a few days.'

'How come you're not at work this morning?'

'We don't open 'til eleven.'

'And what time do you close?'

'Seven at night. This is a bookstore, you know. People don't come into bookstores eight o'clock in the morning.'

'Who wrote *Strangers When We Meet*?' Hawes asked, suddenly.

'Don't ask me nothing about books,' Spedino said. 'All I do is run the cash register and keep an eye on everybody to make sure they don't walk out with half the store.'

'Well,' Carella said, 'thanks for stopping by, Spedino. You'd better get to work now. You don't want to be late.'

Spedino rose, his grey fedora in his hands. He looked first at Carella and then at Hawes and then said, 'You still think I'm involved in this, huh?'

'We'll let you know, Spedino.'

'Just do me one favour.'

'What's that?'

'When you call my boss, when you call Mr Hicks, just tell him this is a routine check, will you? Don't make it sound like I done anything.'

'Sure,' Carella said.

Spedino turned to Hawes with his shark grin and, as though taking him into his confidence, said, 'He still don't believe me, your partner.'

Hawes grinned a peculiar shark grin of his own. 'Neither do I,' he said.

Spedino shrugged and went out of the squadroom.

The funny part about Spedino's story was that it seemed to check out. He *was* working in a bookstore called The Bookends in Riverhead, and the owner of the store – a Mr Matthew Hicks – told Carella that Spedino did handle the store's cash and did keep an eye out for petty thefts which, apparently, he was expert at spotting. Hicks paid him a hundred and seventeen dollars after taxes for his duties, and Spedino seemed happy with the job and happy with his wife and happy with his two children, one of whom was married to an accountant, the other of whom was going to college and studying pharmacy.

Carella hung up and relayed the information to Hawes, who nodded grimly and pulled the telephone directory from its drawer in his desk. They found a listing for a Sigmund Reuhr on Bartlett Street, and they checked out a police sedan and drove down there to kill the morning. On the way down, Hawes again brought up the fact that George Lasser had been able to afford a son in a fancy-shmancy prep school and a wife in a private mental institution, all on what a janitor was earning back in 1939.

'Well, where the hell was he getting the money?' Carella answered somewhat testily.

'Hey, what did I do?' Hawes asked, surprised.

'Nothing, nothing,' Carella said. 'This case is beginning to bug me, that's all. If there's one thing I can't stand, it's puzzles.'

'Maybe Mr Reuhr will solve all the puzzles for us,' Hawes said, and smiled.

'I hope so,' Carella said. 'I certainly hope *somebody* will solve all the puzzles.'

Mr Reuhr, as it turned out, wasn't solving any puzzles for them that morning. Mr Reuhr was a man of about sixty-five with a thin wiry frame and a bald head and piercing brown eyes. He was wearing a brown cardigan sweater over a plaid woollen sports shirt and he admitted them to his apartment after they'd identified themselves, and then asked what he could do for them?

'You can tell us all about the crap games in the basement of 4111 South Fifth,' Carella said, laying it right on the line.

'The *what* games?' Reuhr asked.

'Mr Reuhr, we're not in a mood to fool around,' Carella said, figuring he'd come this far already, so what the hell? 'Gambling's only a misdemeanour, but homicide's the worst felony you'd want to get mixed up in. Now how about telling us what you were doing at those games, and who else was there, and why . . .'

'I don't know what you're talking about,' Reuhr said.

'The crap games, Mr Reuhr.'

'I don't know what you're talking about.'

'The murder of George Lasser, Mr Reuhr.'

'I don't know what you're talking about.'

'Okay, I told you we didn't feel like kidding around. Get your hat, Mr Reuhr.'

'Are you arresting me?' Reuhr asked.

'We're going to have a private little line-up, Mr Reuhr. We're going to walk you in front of another dice player, and ask him to identify you. How about that, Mr Reuhr?'

'I hope you know there are laws in this city against false arrest,' Reuhr said.

'Oh? Are you a lawyer, Mr Reuhr?'

'I've done work for law firms.'

'What kind of work?'

'Accounting.'

'Do you have your own firm, or do you work for someone?'

'I'm retired now,' Reuhr said. 'I used to work for Cavanaugh and Post here in the city.'

'Good. In that case, you won't be losing any time.'

'I want to call a lawyer,' Reuhr said.

'Mr Reuhr, we are not arresting you,' Carella said. 'We are asking you politely to accompany us to the precinct, a request which is within our rights as police officers investigating a murder. Once we get to the station, we will hold you only a reasonable length of time before either releasing you or booking you on a specific charge. All legal and nice, Mr Reuhr.'

'What's a *reasonable* length of time?' Reuhr asked.

'There are several people we have to contact,' Carella said. 'As soon as they arrive, we'll have our line-up, okay? It shouldn't take very long at all.'

'I'm going with you under protest,' Reuhr said, and he put on his coat.

'Mr Reuhr,' Carella advised him, 'this is not a baseball game.'

When they got back to the squadroom, Carella called Danny

Gimp and told him he had picked up Reuhr and was thinking of picking up Spedino as well.

'How come?' Danny asked.

'I want your contact to identify them.'

'Why? Did they say they weren't at those games?'

'That's right.'

'They're full of it. This was straight goods, Steve. The guy I got it from had no reason to snow me.'

'Okay, would he be willing to come up here and identify them?'

'I don't know. He didn't realize he was handing this info to the cops, you dig?'

'Well, break the news to him, will you?'

'I still don't think he'd come up, Steve.'

'We can always pinch him.'

'That'd louse me up just dandy. Besides, it's academic.'

'What do you mean?'

'You want to pinch him, you'll have to get extradition papers.'

'Why? Where is he?'

'He went down to Puerto Rico Saturday.'

'When's he coming back?'

'When the season's over. After Easter.'

'That's great,' Carella said.

'I'm sorry.'

'Argh, the hell with it,' Carella said, and hung up. He stared at the phone for several moments and then went through the gate in the wooden railing and walked down the corridor to where Hawes was waiting with Reuhr in what was loosely called the Interrogation Room. He opened the frosted glass door, went into the room, sat on the edge of the long table and said, 'I promised a reasonable length of time, right, Mr Reuhr? How long have you been here now? Ten minutes?'

'How much longer will it . . .'

'You can go home,' Carella said. Reuhr looked up at him in surprise. 'Go ahead, you heard me. Go home.'

Reuhr rose without saying a word. He put on his hat and coat, and walked out of the room.

The call from Detective-Lieutenant Sam Grossman came at two-thirty that afternoon. A blustery wind was blowing in over

Grover Park, lashing the meshed squadroom windows, whistling under the eaves of the old building. Carella listened to the roar of the wind and beneath that, like a warm breeze from some-where South, the gentle voice of Sam Grossman.

'Steve, I may have something on this axe murder,' Grossman said.

'Like what?' Carella asked.

'Like a motive.'

For a moment, Carella was silent. The window panes rattled beneath a new furious gust of wind.

'What did you say?' he asked Grossman.

'I said I think I may have a motive.'

'For the killing?'

'Yes, for the killing. What did you think? Of course, for the killing. Did you think for the bar-mitzvah?'

'I'm sorry, Sam. This case has been . . .'

'Okay, you want to hear this, or not? I'm a busy man.'

'Shoot,' Carella said, smiling.

'I think the motive is robbery,' Grossman said.

'Robbery?'

'Yeah. What's the matter with you? You going a little deaf or something? Robbery is what I said.'

'But what was there to rob in that basement?'

'Money,' Grossman said.

'Where?'

'Can I tell it in sequence?'

'Sure, go ahead,' Carella said.

'We don't usually like to mess around with deduction here at the lab,' Grossman said. 'We leave that to you masterminds who are out in the field. But . . .'

'Yeah, masterminds,' Carella said.

'Listen, would you mind not interrupting?'

'Go ahead, go ahead,' Carella said. 'I'm sorry, sir, terribly sorry, believe me. I mean that sincerely, sir.'

'Yeah, up yours, too,' Grossman said. 'I'm trying to tell you that Cotton's call set off a train of thought down here, and I think it all adds up now.'

'Let's hear it,' Carella said.

'Well, there's a workbench near the furnace, I guess you saw that.'

'Over behind the coal bin?'

'I think so. You'd be better at locating it than I. All I've got is pictures. You were down there.'

'Well, go ahead, Sam.'

'Okay. There are three shelves over the workbench. They're crammed with jars and tin cans, all of which are full of screws, nuts, bolts, nails, the usual junk you expect to find near a workbench. They're also full of dust.'

'Cotton's told me all this,' Carella said.

'Right. Then you also know that two shelves are covered with dust, but shelf number three, the middle one, has been wiped clean.'

'Why?'

'Well, what's the obvious reason?'

'Fingerprints.'

'Sure. Every schoolboy knows that. So I send John Di Mezzo down for another look, with instructions to study each and every jar and can on that shelf. Johnny does. He's a very good man.'

'And?'

'Why did I ask him to study those jars and cans?' Grossman asked.

'What is this? A police quiz?'

'I'm checking up,' Grossman said.

'Because you figured if somebody wiped that shelf, he must have been after something *on* the shelf and – once he got it – was afraid he'd left prints behind. Since the shelf contained only jars and cans, what he was after must have been *in* the jars or cans.'

'Brilliant,' Grossman said.

'Elementary,' Carella answered.

'In any case, Johnny goes over that middle shelf very carefully and discovers that most of the jars and cans on it are also covered with a layer of nice basement dust. Except one. This single can has been wiped clean, too, just like the shelf. Maxwell House.'

'What?'

'The can. It was a Maxwell House coffee can.'

'Oh. Is that important?'

'No, but I thought you might be interested. In any case, Johnny figures maybe we'd better get that can down here and give it a onceover. So he wraps it carefully and lugs it downtown and we've been going over it. It was full of nuts and bolts and screws and whatnot, you know, just like everything else on the shelf. But after examining it, we have reason to believe the nuts and bolts and junk were put in the can *after* it was wiped clean. Which brings up the possibility that the can contained something else before it was wiped.'

'Hold it, hold it, you're losing me,' Carella said.

'I'll start from the beginning,' Grossman said. 'Middle shelf wiped clean of dust, got it?'

'I've got it.'

'Maxwell House coffee can wiped clean of dust, got it?'

'Got . . .'

'But full of nuts and bolts and junk.'

'Got it.'

'Okay. We empty the can of nuts, bolts, junk, and what do we find.'

'What?'

'The *inside* of the can is wiped spotlessly clean, too. Why bother wiping the inside of the can if the can is full of junk?'

'Why indeed?' Carella asked.

'Because it *wasn't* full of junk. That was put in *after* the can was wiped.'

'What *was* it full of?'

'You want my guess? Money.'

'Anything to back that?'

'Not a thing. Except your own report on the dead man. You said he picked up extra money by selling firewood to some of the tenants in the building.'

'That's right.'

'Well, it's conceivable he kept his receipts in an old coffee can in the basement.'

'Come on, Sam. How much money could he have had in there? A couple of bucks?'

'I know I don't have to remind you of the many murders that have been committed for a couple of *cents* in this fair city of ours.'

'No, you don't have to remind me.'

'Okay. I'm suggesting to you, Steve, that somebody took something out of that can, and that most likely the something was money. Then, in all probability, the thief remembered all those movies he'd seen about leaving fingerprints behind, so he wiped off the can inside and out, and then figured an empty can would look pretty funny on a shelf with full cans. So he reached into all of the cans on the other shelves, taking a few nuts from this one, a few bolts from that one until he had enough to fill the coffee can. Then he wiped off the shelf for good measure.'

'Not too smart, is he?' Carella said.

'No, not too smart,' Grossman answered. 'Who says murderers have to be smart? That's for the comic books. This particular murderer was pretty stupid, in fact. He wipes off *one* can and *one* shelf, leaving the others all covered with dust. He couldn't have caught our attention more effectively if he'd erected a big neon arrow over the workbench.'

'Maybe he *wanted* to catch our attention,' Carella suggested.

'Uh-uh.'

'How do you know?'

'Because he made another mistake.'

'Which was?'

'After all his careful wiping and dusting, he left a goddamn fingerprint on the can.'

'What!'

'Yeah, how about that?'

'Where?'

'On the rim. Part of a thumb print. He probably left it when he was putting the can back on the shelf.'

'Can you get it over to me right away?'

'I've already checked it through B.C.I., Steve. No make.'

'What about the F.B.I.?'

'I can send it directly from here,' Grossman said. 'Save a little time.'

'I'd appreciate it.' Carella paused. 'Maybe I ought to go down and take a look at the basement again myself,' he said.

'You can't lose anything,' Grossman said.

'What do you figure came first? The robbery or the murder?'

'You're buying my theory?'

'I'm buying anything anyone is selling these days,' Carella said, and smiled. 'What do you think the chronology was?'

'I don't know. Maybe the murder came first. That would

explain the mistakes. Our man might not be so stupid after all. Maybe he simply panicked after the murder.'

'You think he knew where that money was kept?'

'No sign of any ransacking, so he must have known.'

'Mm.'

'What do you think, Steve?'

'I'll tell you something,' Carella said. 'For an eighty-seven-year-old cockuh . . . excuse me, do you understand Yiddish?'

'Yeah, yeah, I understand Yiddish,' Grossman said.

'For an eighty-seven-year-old cockuh, this Lasser is sure turning out to be a mystery man.'

'*Everybody's* a mystery man,' Grossman said philosophically. 'It takes murder to bring out all the hidden elements, that's all.'

'Well, thank you anyway for a nice alley to explore and a nice fingerprint to compare against a suspect, if we ever *get* a suspect. Thank you very much, Sam.'

'Don't mention it,' Grossman said. 'And don't worry. You'll crack this one, too.'

'You think so, Sam?'

'Of *course*, I think so! What do you think's going to happen? The *bad* guy's going to win? Don't be ridiculous!'

eight

On Tuesday morning, Cotton Hawes went downtown to 1107 Ganning Street where the accounting firm called Cavanaugh and Post maintained its offices. Sigmund Reuhr had told the detectives he'd once been an accountant with that firm, and Hawes went there in an attempt to learn a little more about the respectably retired, sixty-five-year-old man who attended crap games in slum basements and who lied about them later.

Uptown, in a slum basement, one cop missed death by four inches and another cop missed staying alive by four inches.

The person Hawes spoke to in the firm of Cavanaugh and Post was none other than Mr Cavanaugh himself, who was a portly gentleman with a handlebar moustache and a florid complexion. Sitting opposite him, Hawes found it difficult to accept Cavanaugh as an American businessman who had been born in Philadelphia and raised on that city's brotherly South Side. Cavanaugh resembled a colonel of English cavalry, and Hawes fully expected him to yell 'Charge!' at any moment, and then push on to storm the Turkish bastions.

'You want to know about Siggie, huh?' Cavanaugh said. 'Why? Is he in some kinda trouble?'

'None at all,' Hawes said. 'This is a routine check.'

'What does that mean?'

'What does what mean?' Hawes said.

'A routine check. What do you mean by "routine check"?'

'We're investigating a murder,' Hawes said flatly.

'You think Siggie killed somebody?'

'No, that's not what we think. But certain aspects of our information don't seem to jibe, Mr Cavanaugh. We have reason to believe Mr Reuhr is lying to us, which is why we felt we should look into his background somewhat more extensively.'

'You talk nice,' Cavanaugh said appreciatively.

Hawes, embarrassed, said, 'Thank you.'

'No, I mean it. Where I was raised, if you talked that way you got your head busted. So I talk this way. I got one of the biggest accounting firms in this city, and I sound like a bum, don't I?'

'No, sir.'

'Then what do I sound like?'

'Well, I don't know.'

'A bum, right?'

'No, sir.'

'Okay, we won't argue. Anyway, you talk nice. I like a guy who talks nice. What do you want to know about Siggie?'

'How long did he work here?'

'From 1930 until just last year when he retired.'

'Was he honest?' Hawes asked.

'Right away he hits the bulls-eye,' Cavanaugh said.

'What do you mean?'

'Though I wouldn't say he was *dis*honest,' Cavanaugh said. 'Not exactly, anyway.'

'Then what?'

102

'Siggie likes the horses.'

'A gambler, huh?'

'Mmmm, a gambler like nobody's business. Horses, cards, dice, football games, prize fights, you name it, Siggie's got a bet on it.'

'Did this affect his work in any way?'

'Well . . .' Cavanaugh said, and then shrugged.

'Was he in debt?'

'Once that I know of.'

'When?'

'1937.' Again, Cavanaugh shrugged. 'Listen, almost everybody in this city was in debt in 1937.'

'Was this a gambling debt?'

'Yeah. He was in a poker game and he lost three thousand dollars.'

'That's a lot of money,' Hawes said.

'Even *today* it's a lot of money,' Cavanaugh said. 'In 1937, it was a *hell* of a lot of money.'

'What happened?'

'The guys who were in the game with him took his I.O.U. He had something like sixty days to meet the bill. You've got to understand that these were tough customers. I'm not trying to excuse what Siggie done, I'm only trying to explain that he was in a tight jam.'

'What'd he do? Dip into the company till?'

'Hell, no. What gave you that idea?'

'I thought that's where you were leading.'

'No.'

'Then what happened, Mr Cavanaugh?'

'He tried to shake down a client.'

'Reuhr did?'

'Yeah. He was working on the books for one of our clients and he tipped to a sort of a swindle. What it was, the company was doing some price-fixing, and he threatened to report it unless they paid him off.'

'That's blackmail, Mr Cavanaugh.'

'Well, not exactly.'

'Yes, *exactly*. What happened?'

'The client called me. I told them to forget about it, and then I had a long talk with Siggie. I ended up lending him the three grand, but I also got a promise from him that he'd never pull anything like that again.' Cavanaugh paused. 'Look, can I level with you?'

'Sure.'

'Off the record? I know you're a cop, but you're not a T-man, so let's talk straight for just a minute, okay?'

'Go ahead,' Hawes said.

'You didn't say it was off the record yet.'

'If I say it, will that make it binding?'

Cavanaugh grinned. 'Well, at least we'd have a verbal agreement.'

'Verbal agreements aren't worth the paper they're written on,' Hawes said. 'Samuel Goldwyn, circa 1940.'

'Huh?' Cavanaugh asked.

'Go ahead,' Hawes said. 'Off the record.'

'Okay. In our business, in accounting, there's a lot we see and a lot we forget we ever saw, you know what I mean? You'd be surprised how many cockeyed books in this city suddenly become balanced when it gets near tax time. My point is, I can't afford to have some creep in the organization who goes around finding things in my clients' books and then tries to shake them down. Word like that gets around very fast, you know. So I talked to Siggie like a brother. Siggie, I said, you're a young man – he *was* a young man at the time, this was back in 1937, you know – Siggie, you're a young man, and you've got a future with this company. Now, I know you like the nags, Siggie – still talking to him like a brother – and I know you sometimes get in over your head with gambling debts and this causes you to do crazy things. But Siggie, I was born and raised on Philadelphia's South Side, and that's a very rough neighbourhood, Siggie, just as rough as any of these guys you get into card games with. I'm going to lend you the three grand to pay off your friends, Siggie – still talking like a brother – but I'm going to start deducting ten bucks a week from your pay check until the three grand is paid back, you understand? More important though, Siggie, I learned a few tricks when I was a kid living in Philadelphia and, Siggie, if you ever try to shake down any more of my clients, Siggie, you are going to end up in the River Harb with a base made of solid concrete. Nothing is worse for the accounting business than some creep who has a long nose, Siggie, so cut it out, Siggie, this is fair warning.'

'Did he cut it out?'

'Damn right, he did.'

'How do you know?'

'Look, I know my clients. If anybody from this firm was trying a shakedown, bang, the telephone would ring the next second. No, no. Siggie kept his nose clean from then on. Never another complaint from nobody.'

'That's a little odd, isn't it?'

'Odd? How?'

'Well, unless he kept winning from then on.'

'No, he still lost every now and then. Listen, there ain't a gambler alive who wins *all* the time.'

'Then how'd he meet his debts?'

'I don't know.'

'Mmm,' Hawes said.

'Was there gambling involved in this murder?' Cavanaugh asked.

'Sort of.'

'Well,' Cavanaugh said, 'there's a lot of things I wouldn't put past Siggie Reuhr, but murder ain't one of them. How was the guy killed?'

'With an axe.'

'Blood, you mean?'

'What?'

'Was there lots of blood around?'

'Yes.'

'Then forget Siggie. If it was poison, well maybe. That's more Siggie's speed. But an axe? Blood? Siggie would faint dead on the spot if he got a little cut on his finger from the edge of a ledger. No, sir. If somebody got killed with an axe, it wasn't Siggie Reuhr who killed him.'

One of the cops who visited the basement at 4111 South Fifth that Tuesday morning was Steve Carella.

In the summertime, a city street is a very public place. Most of the citizens are outdoors trying to catch a breath of fresh air, windows are wide open, sounds are magnified, there is a commerce between street and building that does not exist in the winter. Even the melting tar in the gutters seems to echo this pattern of merger, this blending anonymity that is truly the worst thing about a slum dwelling: the person who lives in a tenement is denied many of the pleasures of life and most of its luxuries; he has never known complete privacy, the biggest luxury of them all, but in the summertime he is denied even a semblance of privacy.

Things are a little better in January.

There is privacy inherent in a heavy winter coat pulled up around the back of your neck, there is privacy in your pockets, deep and snug and warm with the heat of your hands. There is privacy in the vestibule of a building with a hissing radiator, there is privacy under the big dining-room table that you bought when you first came from Puerto Rico, there is privacy somehow in the contained heat of a kitchen alive with cooking aromas, there is privacy in a hurried sidewalk conversation with someone you know, the words brisk and to the point, vapour pluming from swiftly moving lips, talk fast, honey, it's goddamn cold out here.

Mrs Whitson, the coloured woman who did the windows and floors at 4111 South Fifth, whose son Sam Whitson had chopped firewood for the late George Lasser at that same address, was standing on the sidewalk having a private, hurried conversation with an elderly man in blue overalls when Carella came down the street. Carella could not hear what they were saying, but he knew that Mrs Whitson had recognized him because she gave a slight jerk of her head in his direction and the man she was talking to turned and looked at Carella and then went back to the conversation. As Carella approached, Mrs Whitson said, 'Hello there. You're the detective, aren't you?'

'Yes, Mrs Whitson,' Carella said.

'Well, well, he remembers my name,' she said, again with that defiant thrust of jaw and chin, that challenging look in her eyes that said nobody was going to stop her from going to any damn school she wanted to.

'I never forget a lady's name, Mrs Whitson,' Carella said, and for a second only the fire left her eyes, for a second only she was simply a skinny hard-working woman who'd had an honest compliment paid her by a good-looking young man.

'Thank you,' she said. Her eyes locked with Carella's.

106

He smiled and said, 'You're welcome.'

'I was just talking to Mr Iverson,' she said. Her eyes did not leave Carella's face. A brooding suspicion had suddenly come into those eyes, almost against the old lady's will, almost through force of habit, you've kicked my goddamn people around for a hundred years, my grandfather was a slave who got beaten regularly with a cat o' nine tails, and now you call me a lady and come buttering me up, who are you after now? my son? what are you going to take from me next, my son Sam who never harmed a butterfly? 'Do you know Mr Iverson?'

'I don't think so,' Carella said. 'How do you do? I'm Detective Carella.'

'How do you do?' Iverson said, and he extended his hand.

'Mr Iverson is the super of the building next door,' Mrs Whitson said. 'I was just talking to him about some work for Sam.'

'Mrs Whitson thought maybe he could chop wood for me again now,' Iverson said.

'Did he used to chop wood for you?' Carella asked.

'Oh, sure, even before Lasser had the idea. I got tenants with fireplaces, too, you know.'

'*Some* fireplaces in these buildings,' Mrs Whitson said. 'They're these old things, they fill the room up with smoke the minute they're lit.'

'They keep the rooms warm, though,' Iverson said.

'Sure. But if you don't die of the cold around here, you die from the smoke.'

She burst out laughing, and both Carella and Iverson laughed with her.

'Well, send him around to see me,' Iverson said when the laughter had subsided. 'Maybe we work something out like before.'

'I'll send him.' Mrs Whitson said, and waved to him as he walked away. As soon as he was out of earshot, she lifted her face to Carella's and looked directly into his eyes and asked, 'You after my son?'

'No, Mrs Whitson.'

'Don't lie to me.'

'I'm not lying to you. I don't think your son had anything to do with the murder of George Lasser.'

Mrs Whitson kept staring at Carella. Then she gave a quick simple nod and said, 'Okay.'

'Okay,' Carella said.

'Then why you here?'

'I wanted to look at the basement again.'

'If you gonna look at it,' Mrs Whitson said, 'you better do it before we both freeze to death out here.' She smiled. 'You know the way?'

'I know the way,' he said.

The man named Kaplowitz met him just outside the door to the basement.

'My name is Kaplowitz,' he said. 'Who are you, and what do you want here?'

'My name is Carella,' Carella answered, showing his shield. 'I want to go down to the basement and look around.'

Kaplowitz shook his head. 'Impossible.'

'Why?'

'I just hosed the basement an hour ago.' Kaplowitz shook his head. 'Dirty basements I seen. Believe me, dirty basements I seen plenty in my day. But a dirty basement like this? Never! Never in my whole life. Two days I'm working on this job now two days since Mr Gottlieb hired me. Two days I go down that basement, I *live* in that basement practically, I look around it, I say, "Kaplowitz, this is *some* dirty basement." Two days, I stand it. But this morning, no more can I stand it. "Kaplowitz," I say, "are you a janitor or a shlub?" I'm a janitor, that's what I am, Kaplowitz the *Janitor*! And such a dirty basement I can't stand. So I took out all the stuff from the tenants, it shouldn't get wet, and I put over the coal some tarpaulin, it shouldn't get wet, and then I connected the hose and *pisssshhhhhhh*, all over the floor! I cleaned everything, everything! Under, over, on, up, down, everything! *Pissshhhh* behind the garbage cans, *pissshhhh* under the workbench, *pissshhhh* near the furnace, *pissshhhh* behind the wash machine and the sink, *pissshhhh* down the drain, everything cleaned up by Kaplowitz the Janitor! So you can't go downstairs now.'

'Why not? If it's all clean . . .'

'It's still wet,' Kaplowitz said. 'You want I should get foot-prints on the floor?'

'Did you spread newspapers?' Carella asked, smiling.

'Ha, ha, very funny,' Kaplowitz said. 'Newspapers I only spread on shabiss.'

'How long will it take to dry?' Carella asked.

'Look, mister,' Kaplowitz said, 'don't rush it, huh? For a hundred years, this basement wasn't washed down. So it finally got cleaned, let it take its time drying, okay? Give it a break, huh? Be a nice man, go take a walk around the block a few times, when you come back the basement will be nice and clean, you'll hardly recognize it.'

'Okay,' Carella said. 'Ten minutes.'

'Fifteen.'

'Ten,' Carella said.

'What are you doing? Bargaining with me? You think because you say ten the floor will listen and dry in ten? Fifteen minutes, okay? Everything will be nice and dry, you can go downstairs and get it all dirty again, okay?'

'Fifteen minutes,' Carella said, and he went out of the building and to the candy store on the corner where he had a cup of coffee. He called the squadroom to ask if there had been any messages and Bert Kling told him Hawes had called to say he was going directly to Cavanaugh and Post from his house. Carella thanked him and then went back to the building. Kaplowitz was nowhere in sight. He went to the rear of the ground floor, opened the door, and paused at the top of the basement steps.

The basement was silent except for the enclosed roar of the furnace and the occasional clatter of overhead pipes. He came down the steps into darkness – there seemed to be a light burning farther back in the basement, but it did not help to illuminate the steps. He groped for the hanging string on the overhead light bulb and pulled at it. The bulb swung, as he released the string, back and forth on its electric wire, casting huge arcs of light on the grey basement wall and the workbench, darkness again, light, darkness, until finally the bulb hung almost motionless, casting a wide circle on the grey concrete floor and the workbench beyond, with darkness beyond that. The next pool of light was farther back in the basement, cast by a second hanging bulb over the sink and drain.

The smell of disinfectant was in his nostrils; Kaplowitz had done a good job.

He moved towards the workbench near the coal bin and felt the sudden sharp wind on his face and thought at first that someone had left a window open. He stepped out of the circle of light, walking into darkness towards the source of the draught. He stepped into the second pool of light near the washing machine and the sink and the drain set in the concrete floor, and then beyond that into darkness again. There seemed to be natural light coming from somewhere at the far end of the basement. He walked towards the light, surprised to find an outside door. He had thought the only entrance was the one behind the steps on the ground floor, inside the building. But as he approached the glass-panelled door at the far end of the building, he realized that it led to a short flight of steps and then into the alleyway at the end of which was the toolshed. George Lasser had kept his axe in that toolshed.

The door was open.

Carella closed the door and wondered if the wind had blown it open. There was no lock on the door, and it closed into the jamb loosely; it was entirely possible that the wind had blown it open. He moved away from the door and began walking back towards the workbench. For a brief and frightening moment, he thought he saw something move in the shadows and his hand went automatically towards his holster. He stopped walking, his hand hovering over the pistol butt. He heard nothing, he saw nothing. He waited for perhaps another thirty seconds and then walked back towards the circle of light near the workbench.

The man in the shadows was holding a monkey wrench in his right hand. He watched Carella and he waited.

Carella studied the workbench, noting everything Grossman had pointed out, noting the spot on the shelf where the Maxwell House coffee can had been resting before the lab boys confiscated it, and then backing away. On impulse, and because cops like to look *under* things as well as on top of them, Carella dropped to his knees and looked under the workbench, but if anything had ever been on the floor under the bench, Kaplowitz's hose had washed it away. Carella got to his feet again; the knees of his trousers weren't even faintly dusty.

The man waited in the shadows near the sink.

Carella turned and began walking towards the sink.

The man's grip on the heavy monkey wrench tightened. He had grabbed the wrench from behind the sink where it was kept for plumbing emergencies. He had grabbed the wrench only seconds after he'd replaced the cover on the drain in the floor, and he had replaced the cover only seconds after he'd heard the basement door opening and the footsteps approaching. He had moved too quickly. The cover was not resting squarely on the drain. If someone tripped over it . . .

Carella kept walking towards the sink.

His foot came within four inches of kicking the metal drain cover. If his foot had connected, he would have become aware of the cover and most probably would have bent to examine it, and he would then have had his head crushed in with a monkey wrench. But his foot missed the drain cover by four inches, and he kicked nothing, and stooped to examine nothing, and therefore had nothing come down on his skull. He looked into the sink, and then went to the washing machine and' opened the door and looked in, expecting to find God knew what, and then sighed and put his hands on his hips. He sighed again.

The man in the shadows waited.

Carella shrugged and then walked to the basement steps. He climbed the steps, turned off the light when he was on the second step from the top, opened the door, went out of the basement and closed the door behind him.

The man did not move from the shadows near the sink.

He waited.

He decided to count to a hundred before he came out. He would count to a hundred, yes, and then lift the cover from the drain again, and then reach into it, he knew exactly where it was caught, there on the flat part before the cement dipped into the hole that carried the water away. He would count to a hundred, just to make sure that cop wasn't coming back. He had thought he was gone that first time, too, when he'd seen him leaving the building. This time, he would make sure.

He had reached fifty-seven, counting slowly, when the door at the top of the staircase opened and the second policeman entered the basement.

The second policeman was in uniform.

The second policeman was a man named Ralph Corey, and he had his own reasons for coming down to the basement this morning, and he had no idea that four inches was going to cost him his life. Corey had been waiting for the opportunity to get down here ever since Carella had spoken to him a week ago

Monday, but there was always somebody down here, either the lab boys or the goddamn police photographers, or newspaper reporters, or what had you. Corey was very anxious to get down here because George Lasser had given him twenty-five dollars every time there was going to be a crap game in the basement of the building, ten of which Corey passed on to the patrolmen, and fifteen of which he kept for himself. But after his talk with Carella, Corey had remembered a peculiar habit of George Lasser's, and it was this habit that had caused his anxiety about getting down to the basement. He remembered talking to Lasser once near the workbench in the basement on the afternoon of one of the crap games, remembered that Lasser had been jotting down some figures in a small black book as Corey had come down the basement steps. As it turned out, Lasser was simply tallying his wood-business receipts, and Corey had put the entire thing out of his mind until that Monday a week ago when Carella started turning the screws. It was then that Corey remembered those figures written in that little black book, all in Lasser's clean, meticulous hand, one under the other in a neat column:

Mrs. Gorman   (3C, 4111) $2.00   12/15
Mrs. Albertson   (1A, 4111)   .50   12/19
Mrs. Carmichael (4A, 4113) $6.00   12/22
Mrs. DiNagro   (2B, 4113) $4.00   12/22

And it was then that Corey began wondering whether neat, meticulous methodical George Lasser who wrote down all these chintzy little log receipts, two bucks, a half a buck, six bucks, whether George Lasser didn't *also* keep a record of *expenditures*, especially when they came in twenty-five dollar lumps every time there was a crap game. And he began wondering whether there was a place in that black book where it said, in Lasser's meticulous little hand:

Corey $25.00   11/7
Corey $25.00   11/16
Corey $25.00   12/4

and so on.

Corey groped along the wall for a light switch, found none, and decided there must be a hanging light with a pull cord. He swung his arms over his head, hitting the bulb with his hand, steadying it, finding the cord, and turning on the light.

The basement was still.

He had seen Lasser making entries in that book at his workbench. That was where he headed now.

He had been a cop for too long a time not to know that there was something very peculiar in this basement. Something warned him of this peculiarity almost at once, something caused the hackles to rise on the back of his neck, and he did not know what the something was until he approached the workbench. One glance told him that a can, or a container of some kind, had been removed from the neatly lined-up cans and jars on the middle shelf, and he wondered if that can – or whatever it had been – was the one in which George Lasser had kept his little black book. The hackles on the back of his neck continued to stand out like a porcupine's quills; Ralph Corey was smelling danger, he was smelling death, and he thought he was smelling only possible suspension from the force. He thought the strong odour in his nostrils was the odour of that goddamn Jew Grossman down at the lab who would by now be pawing over the black book with its notations of payments to somebody named Corey, it wouldn't take the wop Carella long to put two and two together from that.

Corey backed away from the bench. His mouth was suddenly dry. From the corner of his eye, he spotted the sink in the farther circle of light, turned, and walked rapidly towards it. As he approached the sink, the toe of his shoe caught the edge of the drain cover, and he nearly stumbled.

'What the hell . . .' he said aloud, and then looked down to see what it was he'd tripped over. Through the metal bars of the drain he could see something lying on the flat section of the concrete well. It caught the light and glittered. For an instant, Corey thought it was money. He had spent half his life on the police force taking money, and this sure as hell looked like more money. If he had reached for this as speedily as he had reached for rakeoffs throughout the course of his career, if he had begun to stoop a moment sooner, his head would have been four inches lower by the time the monkey wrench lashed out. But it took him just a moment to react to the glittering metal caught on the flat portion of the drain, and he was just beginning to bend for it when the wrench moved out of the shadows. The wrench moved swiftly, soundlessly, and powerfully. It cracked Corey's skull wide open and lodged itself in the pulpy brain matter that had two minutes before been concerning itself with possible suspension from the force.

The man who had wielded the wrench pulled it from Corey's open skull and walked with it towards the trash barrel near the coal bin, dripping blood as he walked. He fished a newspaper from the barrel and wiped the head of the wrench clean of blood. There was no blood on the handle, but he was certain he had left some fingerprints there. He reversed the position of the wrench, holding the jaws with one sheet of newspaper and wiping the bloodless handle clean with another sheet. He looked down and saw that some blood had dripped onto his shoes when he carried the wrench to the barrel, so he took another clean sheet of newspaper and wiped off the few droplets and then carried all of the soiled newspapers to the furnace door, which he opened. He threw the papers inside and waited for them to catch fire before he closed the furnace door.

He threw the cleaned wrench into the trash barrel, and walked back to the sink. Stooping, he lifted the drain cover, and picked up the object that had cost Ralph Corey his life.

The object was a brass button.

Well, now a cop was dead.

Before this, only a janitor was dead.

But now a cop was dead.

There was a big difference.

In order to understand what it is like when a cop gets killed, you must first realize that only two kinds of people kill cops; maniacs and dopes. A maniac is not responsible for anything he does, and a dope is too dumb to know what he is doing. Anybody in his right mind does not go around killing cops. Anybody who can add two and two does not go around killing cops. It is not done. It is crazy and it is stupid. Besides, it is useless. If you kill one cop, there is always some other cop who will take his place, so what's the use? All it does is get everybody all riled up, and it puts the heat on for no good reason, especially in January

114

when you should be under the covers with some nice warm broad, dreaming about going down to Miami. Who needs a dead cop in January to stink up the place and get everybody excited?

Live cops are bad enough.

Dead cops are the world's worst.

There wasn't a single cop in the 87th Precinct who liked, admired, respected or trusted the dead cop who had once been Sergeant Ralph Corey.

That didn't matter.

The way most of them figured it, somebody had been inconsiderate enough to shove a monkey wrench into Corey's head when probably all he was doing was a little investigating into the murder of that janitor a while back. If a poor, hardworking civil servant couldn't go down into a basement to do a little investigation on his own time, they figured, without getting his head bashed in, well, this goddamn city was sure coming to a pretty pass. If you allowed everybody in this goddamn city to go around bashing in a cop's head whenever he got the *urge* to, they figured, just whenever he got the goddamn *urge* to go bashing some cop's head in, well, things were sure getting pretty dangerous for civil servants. And if you just sat back and allowed this goddamn city to fall to pieces that way, people picking up monkey wrenches on every street corner and letting the nearest traffic cop have it right in the eye, well, boy, that was *some* state of affairs. You just couldn't let hordes of people run wild in the streets waving monkey wrenches over their head, and slaughtering anything in a blue uniform, you simply couldn't let that happen because chaos would ensue, no, sir, you couldn't have chaos.

That's the way most of the cops of the 87th figured it.

Also, it was a little scary. Who the hell wants a job where you can get killed?

So almost every cop in the precinct, and hundreds of others throughout the city, filled with righteous indignation, justifiable anger, and a little honest fear, began a personal manhunt for a cop killer. Carella and Hawes didn't know just how this legion of vengeance-seeking men in blue were going to proceed with their search, since hardly any of them knew the facts of the case and only a few of them connected Corey's murder with the murder of George Lasser some ten days before. The detectives supposed

115

that since a cop had been killed, the man who'd murdered him was technically a cop killer. But they rather imagined that Corey's death was simply an extension of the earlier murder and had nothing whatever to do with the fact that he was a cop. This being the case, they couldn't understand what all the goddamn shouting was about. They had been doggedly walking the ass off this homicide since January 3rd, and all of a sudden everyone was getting excited because a crooked cop stopped a monkey wrench.

The only thing that bothered them about Corey's death was the Why of it.

If he had stumbled upon something in that basement, what was it?

Or, discounting the possibility that he had discovered something about the case that was threatening to the killer, what other reason could there have been for his murder? Had he arranged a meeting with someone in that basement? Had he known who the killer was? Was he angling for another payoff, this time one involving homicide?

'There are only two things you can't fix in this city,' someone had told Carella a long time ago, 'and those two things are homicide and narcotics.'

Carella wondered about that now. If a cop will look the other way when a crap game is in progress, if he will look the other way when a citizen from downtown is upstairs banging a prostitute, if he will look the other way when someone passes a traffic light, if he will look the other way often enough, and always for a price – what will stop him from looking the other way, for a price, when a homicide has been committed?

Had Corey been ready to look the other way?

Was his price too high?

Did the murderer figure there was a simpler way to buy Corey's silence? Forever? With no possibility of his returning with another demand?

The possibility existed.

Unfortunately, there were only two people who could tell them whether or not the possibility was a valid one. The first of those people was Ralph Corey, and he was dead. The second was the killer, and they hadn't the faintest idea who he might be.

Wednesday passed.

So did Thursday, somehow.

On Friday, they buried Sergeant Ralph Corey.

Carella's grandmother had always called Friday, 'a hoodoo jinx of a day'. She had not been referring to Friday the Thirteenth, or to any Friday in particular. She was, instead, convinced that *all* Fridays were very bad for human beings, and it was best to avoid them at all costs whenever possible. On Friday, January 17th, the improbable happened.

On Friday, January 17th, Anthony Lasser walked into the squadroom of his own volition and confessed to the murder of his father, George Lasser.

nine

Questioning Tony Lasser was an ordeal neither Hawes nor Carella ever hoped to go through again in their lives, but it was an ordeal that had to be met; the man was, after all, confessing to a murder.

They interrogated him in the squadroom, sitting near the grilled windows with a January wind rattling the panes, the windows themselves rimed, the squadroom clanging with the sound of radiators. Lasser sat trembling in the chair before them. The police stenographer had a bad cold, and besides he was bored, so he kept his eyes glued to his pad without looking up at Lasser who shivered and swallowed and seemed ready to pass out at any moment. The police stenographer sniffed.

'Why'd you kill him?' Carella asked.

'I don't know,' Lasser said.

'You must have had a reason.'

'Yes. Yes, I did.'

'What was it?'

'I didn't like him,' Lasser said, and he shivered again.

'Do you want to tell us what happened, exactly?' Hawes asked.

'What do you want to know?'

'When'd you get the idea to do this?'

'Last week some . . . some time.'

'Last week?' Hawes asked.

'No, no, did I say last week?'

'That's what you said.'

'I meant the week I did it.'

'When was that, Mr Lasser?'

'Before that Friday.'

'Which Friday?'

'The . . . the third, it was. Friday the third.'

'Go on, Mr Lasser.'

'That was when I got the idea to kill him. That week.'

'Around New Year's Eve, would you say?'

'Before then.'

'When? Christmas?'

'Between Christmas and New Year's.'

'All right, Mr Lasser, go ahead. You got the idea, then what?'

'I left the house on Friday, just after lunch.'

'But we thought you never left the house, Mr Lasser?'

Lasser shivered uncontrollably for several moments, his teeth chattering, his hands trembling. He caught hold of himself with great effort and said, 'I . . . I . . . don't usually. This time I . . . I did. To k.k..k . . . kill him.'

'How'd you plan to kill him, Mr Lasser?'

'What?'

'How were you going to kill your father?'

'With the axe.'

'You brought it with you, is that it?'

'No, I . . . I . . . f. . f . . f . . found it when I got there. In the basement.'

'The axe was in the basement?'

'Yes.'

'Where in the basement?'

'Near the . . . furnace.'

'It wasn't outside in the toolshed?'

'No.'

'You knew there'd be an axe there, is that it?'

'What?'

'Had you ever been to that basement before, Mr Lasser?'

'No.'

'Then how'd you know there'd be an axe there?'

'What?'

'Mr Lasser, how did you know there was going to be an axe in that basement?'

'Well, I . . . . I didn't.'

'Then how did you expect to kill your father?'

'I d . . . d . . . didn't think it out that clearly.'

'You were just going to figure it out when you got there, is that right?'

'That's right,' Lasser said.

'Are you getting this, Phil?' Carella asked the stenographer.

'Yop,' the stenographer said, without looking up.

'Go ahead, Mr Lasser,' Hawes said.

'W . . . w . . . what do you want me to tell you?'

'What'd you do after you killed him?'

'I . . . I . . . I . . . I . . .' He could not get past the single word. He swallowed and tried again, 'I . . . I . . . I . . .' but he was shaking violently now, and the word was lodged in his throat. His face had gone pale, and Carella was sure he would either faint or vomit within the next few moments. Painfully, he watched Lasser and wished he could help him.

'Mr Lasser,' he said, 'can I get you some coffee? Would you like something hot to drink?'

'N . . . n . . . no,' Lasser said.

'Mr Lasser, on the day you killed your father, did you react in this way?'

'W . . . wh . . . wha . . .?'

'When you left the house, I mean?'

'No, I wa . . . wa . . . was all right.'

'Mr Lasser . . .' Carella started.

'Mr Lasser,' Hawes interrupted, 'why are you lying to us?'

Lasser looked up suddenly and blinked, and then shivered.

'Why are you telling us you killed your father when you didn't?' Carella said.

'I did!'

'No, sir.'

'I did! Wh . . . what's the matter with you? C . . . c . . . c . . . ca . . .?'

'Take it easy, Mr Lasser.'

'Can't you see I'm t . . . t . . . telling the truth?'

'Mr Lasser, the man who swung that axe was powerful and

deadly and accurate. You're having trouble just staying in that chair. Now . . .'

'I did it,' Lasser said, and then shivered. 'B . . . believe me. I d . . . d . . . d . . . did it.'

'No, Mr Lasser.'

'Yes.'

'No. Why are you here?'

'Because I k . . . k . . . k . . . k . . . k . . .'

He could not say the word. They waited in painful silence while he struggled with it, and finally a shiver rattled his body and he spat out the word as though it were some loathsome creature that had been squatting malevolently on his tongue. *Killed!* he shouted. 'I *killed* my father!'

'In that case, Mr Lasser,' Carella said, 'you won't mind if we check your fingerprints against one we found in the basement, will you?'

Lasser was silent.

'Will you, Mr Lasser?'

He did not answer.

'Mr Lasser,' Hawes said gently, 'why did you leave your house today?'

Lasser suddenly began sobbing. The police stenographer looked up, puzzled, and Carella signalled for him to leave. The stenographer hesitated. Carella touched his elbow and coaxed him out of the chair.

'Don't you want me to take this down?' the stenographer asked.

'No,' Carella said. 'We'll call you if we need you.'

'Okay,' the stenographer said, and he went out of the squad-room, but he was still puzzled. In the straight-backed chair near the frost-whitened windows, Tony Lasser shivered and sobbed.

'What happened, Mr Lasser?' Carella asked.

Lasser shook his head.

'Something must have happened to bring you here, sir.'

Again, Lasser shook his head.

'Won't you please tell us?' Hawes said softly, and Lasser reached for his handkerchief with trembling fingers, and blew his nose, and then, shivering, stuttering, sobbing, told them what had happened.

Someone on that quiet New Essex street with its Tudor

120

reproductions, someone among Tony Lasser's neighbours . . .

'Was it Mrs Moscowitz across the street?' Carella asked.

No, no, Lasser said, no, not Mrs Moscowitz. She was a pain in the neck, but not a malicious woman. No, it was someone else, it didn't matter who, really, just someone in the neighbourhood.

'Yes, go ahead, what happened?' Hawes said.

Well, someone had come to Tony Lasser the day before. The someone was a spokesman for a sort of lynch party, Northern style, except that no one was really going to be hanged or tarred and feathered, not really, not if everyone would 'go along'. That was just the way Lasser's neighbour had phrased it. He had said everything would be fine and dandy and everyone would be satisfied if they would all just 'go along'. Lasser still hadn't the faintest inkling what this neighbour wanted of him. He had been called from his study at the back of the house where he'd been illustrating a children's book about tolerance, and here was this stranger . . . well, practically a stranger . . . whom he'd seen perhaps once or twice from his window, but whom he did not know at all. Now the stranger was talking about going along, and Lasser asked him what he meant.

'Your mother,' the neighbour said.

'My mother?'

'Mmm.'

'Well, what about her?' Lasser asked.

'We want her put away, Mr Lasser.'

'Why?'

'That's the wish of the neighbourhood, Mr Lasser.'

'That's not *my* wish,' Lasser said.

'Well, you haven't got a hell of a lot to say about it, Mr Lasser,' the neighbour said, and then went on to explain the barrel the neighbours had constructed, the barrel over which they felt they now had Tony Lasser.

They had all read about the murder of Lasser's father, and one of the newspapers had mentioned that the axe had been wielded by someone who possessed 'the strength of a madman' or some such journalese which had given them their idea. They had got together and taken a vote and decided that they would go to the police and say they had seen Estelle Lasser leaving her house at about twelve noon on Friday, January third, the day her husband

George was hacked to death in the basement of his tenement building.

'But that isn't true,' Tony Lasser said.

'Yes, but we have two people who will swear that they saw her leaving the house.'

'My mother will say she didn't.'

'Your mother is insane.'

'*I'll* say she didn't,' Lasser said.

'Everybody knows you won't step out of this house,' the neighbour said.

'What has that got to do with . . .?'

'You think they'll take the word of a man who's afraid to go outside? You think they'll take his word over the word of two normal citizens?'

'I'm normal,' Lasser said.

'Are you?' the neighbour asked.

'Get out of my house,' Lasser said in a hushed and deadly whisper.

'Mr Lasser,' the neighbour said, unruffled, 'everything'll work out fine here if we just go along with each other. We're not trying to get anyone in trouble, we're just trying to get a woman who is a maniac . . .'

'She is *not* a maniac!' Lasser said.

'. . . a maniac, Mr Lasser, all we're trying to do is get her out of this neighbourhood and away where she belongs. Now we figure that either you'll voluntarily have her committed, Mr Lasser, or we'll get her involved with the police, call her to the attention of the authorities as it were, have *them* ask her a few questions, do you think she could stand up under a third degree, Mr Lasser? Do we go along, or what?'

'She isn't harming anyone.'

'She's a pain in the ass, Mr Lasser, and we're all sick of apologizing for the maniac who lives on the block.'

'She isn't *harming* anyone,' Lasser repeated.

'Mr Lasser, this is it now, you listening? We're going to give you 'til Monday morning to make up your mind. If you can assure us by then that you've contacted the authorities and your mother will be taken away, why fine, we'll all shake hands and have a drink to our continued good fellowship. If on the other hand, Mr Lasser, we do not hear from you by then, we'll go to the police and say that your mother was out of this house on the day your father was killed. We'll just let them take it from there.'

'That would be lying,' Lasser said. 'My mother was here.'

'Yes, that's right, Mr Lasser. It'd be lying.' The neighbour smiled. 'But a lie ain't a lie no more when somebody swears to it.'

'Get out,' Lasser said.

'Think it over.'

'Get out.'

'Think it over.'

He had thought it over. He had decided that whatever else happened, his mother was not to be institutionalized again. If his neighbours went to the police and cast suspicion on his mother . . . if the police began asking her questions . . . if, God forbid, she lost control . . . they would surely ask for her commitment. He could not allow that to happen. There was one way he could protect her. If he confessed to the crime himself, why then they would leave her alone.

Lasser dried the tears from his eyes.

'That's why I'm here,' he said.

'Okay, Mr Lasser,' Carella said. 'Genero, bring us some coffee!' he yelled.

'I d . . . d . . . don't want any coffee,' Lasser said.

Carella ignored him. When the coffee came, they asked him whether he took it black or with cream and Lasser said he took it black. How much sugar, they asked him, and he said he took it with no sugar. He wanted to get back to his mother, he said. He shouldn't have left her alone for so long.

'Mr Lasser,' Carella said, 'suppose we'd believed your story?'

'What story?'

'That you killed your father.'

'Oh. Yes.'

'Suppose we'd believed you, and suppose you'd gone to trial and been convicted . . .'

'Yes?'

'Mr Lasser, who'd have taken care of your mother?'

Lasser seemed suddenly confused. 'I never thought of that,' he said.

'Mmm. Then it's a good thing we *didn't* believe you, huh?'

'Yes, I guess so.'

'We're going to have a patrolman see you home, Mr Lasser,' Hawes said. 'As soon as you finish your coffee . . .'

'I can get home by myself.'

'We know you can, sir,' Hawes said gently, 'but we'd like to . . .'

'I can take a taxi,' Lasser said.

'It's no trouble at all, believe me, sir,' Hawes said. 'We'll radio for a car . . .'

'I'll take a taxi,' Lasser said. 'I took one here, and I'll take one home. I . . . I . . . I don't want a police car pulling up in . . . in front of the house. There've been enough police since . . . since my . . . my father died.' Lasser paused. 'He was not a bad man, you know. I . . . I . . . was never overly fond of him, I . . . I must say I couldn't cry when I learned he was . . . was . . . d . . . dead, no tears would come, but he was not a bad man. He sent me to a good school, he sent my mother to a private institution, he was not a bad man.'

'How could he afford that, Mr Lasser?' Hawes asked suddenly.

'Afford what?'

'The school. The sanitarium.'

'Well, he had a better job at the time,' Lasser said, and shrugged.

'What do you mean? He was a janitor in 1939, wasn't he?'

'Yes, but in a better building. Not in a slum area.'

'Where?'

'Downtown,' Lasser said.

'Downtown where?'

'At 1107 Ganning, do you know the area?'

'I think so,' Hawes said. 'That's in the financ . . .' and then cut himself short. '1107 *Ganning*, did you say?'

'Yes.'

'Your father was the janitor of 1107 Ganning in 1939?'

'Yes, that's right. What . . . ?'

'Steve,' Hawes said, 'Siggie Reuhr was working for Cavanaugh and Post in 1939.'

'So?'

'At 1107 Ganning Street,' Hawes said.

Sigmund Reuhr was still in bed when the detectives knocked on his door. He asked who it was, and they told him it was the police, and he mumbled something they couldn't understand and

124

then came through the apartment to the front door. sHe wa
belting a blue paisley robe over his red striped pyjamas when he
opened the door for them.

'What now?' he asked. 'Some more Gestapo tactics?'

'Just some questions, Mr Reuhr,' Carella said. 'Mind if we
come in?'

'Would it make any difference if I minded?'

'Sure,' Hawes said. 'If you minded, we'd probably arrest you
and take you uptown and book you. This way, it can all be nice
and friendly, a private little chat without charges or counter-
charges or anything.'

'Yeah, friendly,' Reuhr said, and he led them into the apartment. 'I just got up,' he said. 'I'm going to make some coffee. I
can't talk to anybody until I've had a cup of coffee.'

'Take your time, Mr Reuhr,' Carella said. 'This has been
waiting around since 1939.'

Reuhr shot Carella a quick, suspicious glance, seemed about
to say something, but closed his mouth instead and went into
the kitchen. He fixed his pot of coffee, put it on the stove to
percolate, and then came back into the livingroom. He sat
opposite the detectives, but he did not say a word to them until
his coffee was ready. Then, sipping at it, he asked, 'What did
you mean about 1939?'

'Well, suppose you tell us, Mr Reuhr.'

'I don't know what you're talking about,' Reuhr said.

'Mr Reuhr,' Hawes said, 'we think it is a very big coincidence
that someone says he saw you at a crap game at 4111 South Fifth
in the basement where a man named George Lasser was janitor,
and . . .'

'I don't know what you're talking about.'

'Which is very strange, considering the coincidence.'

'What coincidence?'

'In 1939, when you were working for Cavanaugh and Post at
1107 Ganning Street downtown, the superintendent of that
building was a man named George Lasser. How about that, Mr
Reuhr?'

'So what? I'm an accountant. You think I knew who the super
of the building was?'

'We think you did, Mr Reuhr.'

'You'd have a hell of a time proving it. And, anyway, what if

125

I did? Is there a law against knowing the super of a . . .'

'There is a law against shooting craps, Mr Reuhr,' Hawes said.

'There is also a law against murdering people,' Carella said.

'Argh, bullshit,' Reuhr said. 'I didn't murder anybody, and you know it.'

'Mr Reuhr, we talked to Mr Cavanaugh, one of the partners in the accounting firm for which you worked.'

'So?'

'Mr Cavanaugh told us that in 1937 you attempted to shake down one of his clients, is that true?'

'No.'

'We think it's true, Mr Reuhr.'

'So what? That was in 1937. What's that got to do with today?'

'That's what we're trying to find out.'

'Yeah, well . . .'

'We have a few ideas, Mr Reuhr.'

'I'm not interested in your ideas,' Reuhr said, and he put down his coffee cup. 'In fact, I think we'd better do what you suggested earlier. I'm tired of this little *friendly* chat. I think I'd better get dressed, and you'd better arrest me and take me uptown and book me, okay? I'd like to know what you're going to book me for.'

'How does murder sound, Mr Reuhr?'

'*Whose* murder?'

'George Lasser's murder.'

'Come on, why the hell would I kill George Lasser?'

'Then you *did* know him, huh?'

'Who said so?'

'Mr Reuhr, let's do what you said we should, okay? Go put on your clothes, and we'll take you uptown and book you. *We're* a little tired of this friendly chat, too.'

'Book me for what?' Reuhr asked again.

'Why, murder, Mr Reuhr. I thought we'd told you.'

Reuhr was silent for several moments. 'I didn't kill Georgie,' he said at last.

'*Were* you at those crap games, Mr Reuhr?'

Reuhr nodded. 'Yes.'

'What about Spedino? Did he play, too?'

'Yeah, he was there.'

'Then why'd he lie about it?'

126

'Because his wife would kill him if she knew he was shooting dice.'

'You mean he lied to us, even knowing there was a homicide involved, just because he's afraid of his *wife*?'

'Have you ever met his wife?' Reuhr asked.

'Okay,' Carella said, and shrugged. 'What about George Lasser? Did you know him back in 1939?'

'Yes.'

'What was the extent of your relationship with him?' Carella asked.

'Just hello and good-bye. You know. I'd see him in the hallway every now and then, I'd say "Hello, Georgie, how are . . ." '

'That's a lie, Mr Reuhr,' Carella said.

'Huh?'

'Mr Reuhr, back in 1939 George Lasser was able to afford a prep school for his son Tony and a private mental institution for his wife Estelle. He couldn't have done all that on a janitor's salary, Mr Reuhr. So we made a few guesses, and we're going to try them for size, okay, Mr Reuhr? Just for size, okay? We'll get the right colour later.'

'Are you supposed to be comical?' Reuhr asked.

'No, I'm supposed to be dead serious,' Carella answered. 'We know that George Lasser was an ambitious man constantly on the lookout for fresh angles. We know that you'd already shaken down one of your firm's clients and been warned against attempting the same thing again, and we also know that you and George Lasser worked in the same building at the same time. You've just told us that you knew him, so we . . .'

'Just to say hello to.'

'Sure. We think it was a little more than that, Mr Reuhr.'

'Yeah? What do you think it was?'

'We think you found another one of your firm's clients to blackmail, and . . .'

'I'd watch how you throw around that word blackmail.'

'Never mind what I watch, Mr Reuhr. We think you found another sucker to blackmail, but you knew that Cavanaugh would break you in a hundred pieces if you tried it again. That is, if you tried it again *personally*.' Carella paused. 'Are you beginning to get the picture, Mr Reuhr?'

'I don't know what you're talking about.'

'He never seems to know what we're talking about,' Carella said to Hawes conversationally. 'What we are talking about, Mr Reuhr, is this. We think you found someone who needed blackmailing and, knowing you could not go to him personally decided to send a representative in your place. We think the person you decided to send was George Lasser. That's what we think.'

'Mmm-huh,' Reuhr said.

'What do *you* think, Mr Reuhr?'

'I think that's very interesting.'

'Yes, we do too.'

'But I don't think you can prove any of it.'

'You're right. We can't,' Carella said.

'That's what I thought,' Reuhr said, and smiled.

Carella returned the smile. 'We don't have to, Mr Reuhr,' he said.

'You don't, huh?'

'Nope.'

'How come?'

'We're not interested in something as piddling as blackmail. We're interested in homicide. We've been getting a lot of heat on this, Mr Reuhr. We'd really like very much to find someone to hang it on.'

'You would, huh?'

'Yes, indeed. Why don't we play ball with each other?'

'In what way?'

'Mr Reuhr, we *can't* prove that you and Lasser were blackmailing someone together in 1939, that's true. But we *can* prove blackmail in 1937 because Mr Cavanaugh has already told us all about it, and I'm sure he'd repeat it on the witness stand, and would also tell us the name of your victim. In other words, Mr Reuhr, we've got you for *that* little caper, if for nothing else.'

'Mmm,' Reuhr said.

'Make sense?'

'What's your deal?'

'We don't think you killed Lasser,' Hawes said.

'How come?'

'We can't see any reason for it. From what we can see, you and Lasser were friends. He was in on a shake-down deal with

128

you, let you use the basement for your crap games, why should you kill him?'

'Mmm,' Reuhr said.

'Still make sense, Mr Reuhr?'

'I'm listening,' Reuhr said.

'I think he knows what we're talking about now,' Carella said, and smiled at Hawes.

'Go on,' Reuhr said.

'Okay. You and Lasser are shaking somebody down. Apparently, you're getting quite a bit of loot from this person because Lasser is able to afford the school and the hospital on his share alone. You start the shakedown in 1939 . . .'

'We started it in 1938,' Reuhr said suddenly.

'Ah,' Carella said. 'Thank you. I think he would like to play ball, Cotton.'

'I think so, too,' Hawes said, and grinned.

'You started the shakedown in 1938,' Carella said. 'George Lasser was the man who went to your victim and told him what you had on him. George Lasser was the man who demanded payment.' Carella paused. 'George Lasser was also the man who got killed with an axe on the third of this month. Get it, Mr Reuhr?'

'I think so.'

'We want to know what the shakedown was about and who your victim was,' Hawes said.

Reuhr shrugged. 'What do I get out of this?' he asked.

'*That's* what, Mr Reuhr.'

'Huh?'

'You get *out* of this. You get out of what could be a very nasty situation. You get out of it clean and with no further questions. Otherwise, we still need someone to pin a rose on – and it might turn out to be you.'

'Okay,' Reuhr said.

'See?' Carella said to Hawes. 'He *does* know what we're talking about, after all.'

'The victim?' Hawes asked.

'A man named Anson Burke.'

'What do you have on him?'

'He was president of his company, a firm exporting automobile parts to South America. He came into the office one day and asked if we would prepare his personal income tax return. This was pretty fishy to begin with because his firm had its own accountants, but he was going outside to have his personal tax figured. Anyway, we took him on. That's how I found out about the forty grand.'

'What forty grand?'

'You know anything about the export business?'

'Very little.'

'Well, most of them'll buy the parts they need for export from various suppliers all around the country. The usual deal is for the supplier to give the exporter a flat discount, usually about fifteen per cent.'

'Yeah, go on.'

'Well, every now and then, if the exporter brings the supplier an unusually large amount of business, the supplier'll give an additional discount.'

'How much more?'

'Well, in this case, it was five per cent more. Burke's firm was probably doing business of eight hundred thousand to a million a year with this one supplier alone. You take five per cent of eight hundred thousand, and you've got forty grand.'

'There's that forty grand again,' Hawes said. 'What about it?'

'That's how much he got.'

'Who?'

'Burke.'

'From who?'

'From this supplier in Texas.'

'For what?'

'Well, he listed it as a commission, but it was really that additional five per cent I told you about.'

'I don't understand,' Carella said. 'Listed it where?'

'On the information return he gave me for his personal income tax.'

'He listed forty thousand dollars as a commission from a supplier in Texas, is that it?'

'That's right. He was drawing thirty thousand from his company as salary. This was over and above that.'

'So?'

'So, at least he was smart enough to look for another accountant far away from his regular business accountants.'

'What do you mean, smart?'

'Because the forty thousand bucks was paid to him *personally*. It never went into the firm. He was declaring it on his personal income tax so everything would be nice and legal as far as Uncle Sam was concerned, but he was robbing it from his stockholders.'

'Go on,' Carella said.

'Well, I knew I had something good there if I could only get to him. But how? One peep out of me, and he might have gone to Cavanaugh, and the next thing I knew Cavanaugh would call Philadelphia and talk to some of his childhood friends who were now adult hoods, and I'd be fishing in the River Dix, only from the bottom. Then I remembered talking to Lasser once or twice. I knew he was slightly crooked because he used to steal brass fittings and copper tubing, stuff like that from the basement which he'd later sell to junkyards. Burke's office was all the way over on the other side of town. He didn't know Lasser from a hole in the wall.'

'How'd you set it up?'

'I contacted Lasser and explained the deal to him. He was interested. Then I called Burke and told him I wanted to work on his tax return one day that week, and would he please bring his records to the office, including all the stuff I would need for that year, like his withholding statements and also the information return about that forty thousand dollar commission. He said he would bring it in the next day. I went up that afternoon to work in his private office, and told him to keep the stuff in the city rather than taking it back home with him, because I'd have to come back again tomorrow to finish up. He locked it in the top drawer of his desk.'

'Go on.'

'Lasser and I broke into his office that night. We were after the information return, but to make it look good, we grabbed a gold pen and pencil and some petty cash and a typewriter and some other junk laying around the office. Burke discovered the theft the next morning. Two weeks later, Lasser contacted him.'

'What did he tell him?'

'He confessed to being the man who had broken into the office,

Burke was ready to call the police, but then Lasser showed him the return. He said he had grabbed it by accident with some of the other stuff in the drawer, and that he didn't know very much about the exporting business, but he knew the name of the firm was Anson Burke, Incorporated, and here was an information return going to the United States Government and listing a payment of forty thousand dollars to Anson Burke *personally*, rather than to the firm, and this looked kind of fishy to him. Burke told Lasser to go to hell, and said he was definitely going to call the police now, at which point Lasser apologized and said maybe he was wrong, maybe everything *was* clean and above board, in which case Burke wouldn't mind if Lasser mailed that information return to the company's board of directors. It was then that Burke saw the light. In fact, it damn near blinded him.'

'So he paid Lasser whatever he asked for.'

'Yes.'

'And that was how much?'

'Well, Burke had stolen forty grand that year from the company. Lasser and I figured he'd be stealing at least that, if not more, each and every year we kept quiet about it.'

'Yeah, so?'

'Lasser asked him for half of it.'

'Or else.'

'Yeah. Or else he'd go straight to the board of directors.'

'So Burke paid.'

'Yes.'

'And you and Lasser split twenty grand.'

'That's right. Ten grand each.'

'And you continued to get it each year. That can come to a lot of money,' Carella said. 'So it's entirely possible that Burke finally got fed up with being bled. He went to that basement on South Fifth and killed Lasser in an attempt to free himself of . . .'

'No,' Reuhr said.

'Why not?'

'The golden eggs stopped coming in 1945.'

'What do you mean?'

'No more after 1945,' Reuhr said. 'No more money after then.'

'Burke stopped paying you in 1945? Is that it?'

Reuhr smiled. 'That's right,' he said.

'He still might have been sore about what he'd paid out *up* to

132

that time. He may have finally decided to do something about it.'

'Uh-uh,' Reuhr said, and there was something maliciously gleeful about his smile now.

'Why not?' Carella asked.

'Anson Burke couldn't have killed Lasser.'

'Why not?'

'I just told you. He stopped paying us.'

'So?'

'The reason he stopped paying was that he dropped dead of a heart attack in 1945.'

'What?' Carella said.

Reuhr nodded gleefully. 'Yeah.' Still grinning, he said, 'There goes your ball game, huh?'

January is a lousy month for ball games.

They didn't pinch Sigmund Reuhr because they doubted if they had a real case, and besides – to tell the truth – it was too damn much trouble. Reuhr's victim and Reuhr's partner were both dead, and for the previous blackmail attempt they had only Cavanaugh's word, which might be considered hearsay in court without the corroborating evidence of the intended 1937 victim. The possibility of getting that intended victim to incriminate himself by incriminating Reuhr was exceptionally slim and anyway the whole mess seemed like very small potatoes when there was a homicide kicking around.

January is just a lousy month for ball games, that's all.

When they got back to the squadroom, Detective Meyer met them at the slatted wood railing and said 'Where you guys been?'

'Why?' Carella asked.

'We got a call a few minutes ago. From Murphy on the beat.'

'Yeah?'

'A coloured handyman just tried to kill the super of a building.'

'Where?'

'4113 South Fifth,' Meyer said. 'His name's Sam Whitson.'

ten

There were two patrolmen sitting on Sam Whitson's legs when Carella and Hawes arrived. Another two had pinned down his huge outstretched arms, and yet another cop straddled his chest. The immense Negro gave a sudden lurch into the air, his midsection bucking, as the detectives came closer to where he was pinned to the basement floor. The cop sitting on his chest flew into the air and then grabbed for the lapels of Whitson's Eisenhower jacket and landed again on his chest with a heavy thud.

'You son of a bitch,' Whitson said, and a patrolman standing by and watching the others struggling with their prisoner, suddenly hit Whitson on the sole of his right foot with his nightstick. At one side of the basement, his head bleeding from a cut across the scalp and forehead, sat John Iverson, the superintendent of the building at 4113 South Fifth, next door to 4111 where George Lasser had worked. The buildings were side by side and attached, like two halves of the same embryo. Iverson's basement was a mirror image of Lasser's except for its contents. He sat now on an empty milk crate and nursed his broken head while the patrolmen struggled with Whitson who kept trying to shake them off at regular intervals. The one patrolman who was not engaged in the struggle kept hitting Whitson with his nightstick at regular intervals, too, until finally one of the other cops yelled, 'For Christ sake, Charlie, will you cut it out? Everytime you hit the bastard, he jumps in the air.'

'I'm trying to calm him,' Charlie said, and hit Whitson's shoe sole again.

'Lay off,' Carella said, and he walked to where the cops swarmed over the fallen Negro. 'Let him up.'

'He's pretty dangerous, sir,' one of the patrolmen said.

'Let him up,' Carella repeated.

'Okay, sir,' the spokesman for the patrolmen said, and then they all jumped off Whitson at precisely the same moment, as

134

though by prearranged signal, and backed far away from him as Whitson sprang to his feet with his fists clenched and murder in his eyes.

'It's okay, Sam,' Carella said gently.

'Who says so?' Whitson wanted to know. 'I'm goan kill that son of a bitch.'

'You're not going to kill anybody, Sam. Sit down and cool off. I want to know what happened here.'

'Get outa my way,' Whitson said. 'This ain't none of your affair.'

'Sam. I'm a police officer,' Carella said.

'I know what you is,' Whitson said.

'Okay. I got a call saying you tried to kill the super. Is that right?'

'You goan get another call in jus' a few minutes,' Whitson said. 'It's goan tell you I *did* kill the super.'

Carella, in spite of himself, burst out laughing. The laughter surprised Whitson who unclenched his fists for a moment and stared at Carella with a dumbfounded expression on his face.

'It ain't funny,' Whitson said.

'I know it's not, Sam,' Carella answered. 'Let's sit down and talk it over.'

'He came at me with a goddamn *axe*,' Whitson said, pointing to Iverson.

For the first time since they had come into that basement, Carella and Hawes were fully aware of Iverson as something more than just an innocent assault victim. If Whitson were immense, Iverson was just as large. If Whitson were capable of wreaking havoc, Iverson could easily have caused much the same destruction. He sat on the milk crate with his forehead and scalp bleeding, but the cut did nothing to diminish the feeling of power and strength that emanated from him like the smell of a jungle beast. As Whitson pointed to him, he lifted his eyes and the detectives suddenly sensed his alert tension, a nervous energy that transmitted itself as surely as did his stench of power, so that they themselves approached him with a wariness they would not have ordinarily exercised on a bleeding man.

'What does he mean, Iverson?' Carella asked.

'He's crazy,' Iverson said.

'He just said you came at him with an axe.'

'He's crazy.'

'What's this?' Hawes asked, and he bent to pick up an axe that was lying on the basement floor some ten feet from where Iverson was sitting. 'This looks like an axe to me, Iverson.'

'It *is* an axe,' Iverson said. 'I keep it down here in the basement. I use it for chopping up things.'

'What's it doing on the floor?'

'I must have left it there,' Iverson said.

'He's lying,' Whitson said. 'When he come at me with that axe, I hit him, and he *drop* it there on the floor. *That's* what it's doing on the floor there.'

'What'd you hit him with?'

'I picked up the rake there. I hit him with that.'

'Why?'

'I just told you. He come at me with that axe.'

'Why'd he do that?'

''Cause he a cheap bastard,' Whitson said, 'that's why.'

Iverson got to his feet and took a step towards Whitson. Carella moved between them and shouted, 'Sit down! What does he mean, Iverson?'

'I don't know what he means. He's crazy.'

'Offering me twenty-five cents,' Whitson said indignantly. 'I told him what he could do with his twenty-five cents. Twenty-five cents!'

'What are you talking about, Whitson?' Hawes asked, and then seemed to discover he was still holding the axe in his hands. He propped it against the wall of the coal bin just as Whitson wheeled towards Iverson again.

'Now just *hold* it, goddamn it!' Hawes yelled, and Whitson stopped dead in his tracks. 'What's all this about twenty-five cents?'

'He offered me twenty-five cents to chop his wood. I told him to shove it up his . . .'

'Let me get this straight,' Carella said. 'You wanted him to chop wood for you, is that right, Iverson?'

Iverson nodded and said nothing.

'And you offered him twenty-five cents?'

'Twenty-five an hour,' Iverson said. 'That's what I always paid him before.'

136

'Yeah, and that's why I quit choppin' wood for you, you cheap bastard. That's why I start working for Mr Lasser.'

'But you used to work for Mr Iverson here, is that it?' Hawes asked.

'Las' year, I used to work for him. But he was only paying me twenty-five cents an hour, and Mr Lasser he offers me fifty cents an hour, so I quits here and goes there. I ain't no fool.'

'Is this true, Iverson?'

'I gave him more work,' Iverson said. 'I paid less, but there was more work, more hours.'

'That was only until Mr Lasser start getting all your customers,' Whitson said.

'What do you mean?' Hawes asked.

'All the people here in this building, they starts going next door for they wood. To Mr Lasser.'

They were staring at Iverson now, staring at the huge man with his hands dangling clumsily at his sides, his teeth nibbling at the soft flesh inside his mouth, his eyes wary and alert, a look of animal disarray about him.

'Is this true, Mr Iverson?' Carella asked.

Iverson did not answer.

'Mr Iverson, I want to know if this is true,' Carella said.

'Yes, yes, it's true,' Iverson said.

'That all your customers started going to Mr Lasser for their wood?'

'Yes, yes,' Iverson said. 'That don't mean nothing. It don't mean I . . .'

Iverson cut himself off. The basement was silent.

'What doesn't it mean, Mr Iverson?'

'Nothing.'

'You were about to say something, Mr Iverson.'

'I said all I got to say.'

'Your customers all began going to Mr Lasser, is that right?'

'I told you yes! What do you want from me? My head is bleeding, *he* hit me on the head, why are you asking *me* the questions?'

'How did you feel about that?' Carella asked.

'About what?'

'About your wood customers leaving you?'

137

'I . . . look, I . . . I had nothing to do with it.'

'With what?'

'I was angry, yes, but . . .'

Again, Iverson stopped talking. He stared at Carella and Hawes who were watching him quietly and solemnly. And then, for whatever reasons of his own, perhaps because he felt he could no longer communicate, perhaps because he felt he had walked into a trap and the jaws had closed upon him, his face changed and a decision moved across it as visibly as if it had been stamped there in ink. Without another word, he turned swiftly and reached for the axe Hawes had propped against the side of the bin. He lifted the axe easily and effortlessly, so quickly that Carella barely had time to move out of its path as it swung around like a base-ball bat aimed at his head.

'Duck!' Hawes shouted, and Carella immediately threw himself flat on the floor, rolling over onto his left shoulder as Hawes' shot rang out behind him, reaching for the service revolver in the holster at his hip just as Hawes got off his second shot. He heard someone grunt in pain, and then Iverson was standing over him with a huge blot of blood spreading on the front of his overalls, the axe raised high over his head, the way it must have been raised on that Friday afternoon just before he had finally sunk it into the skull of George Lasser. Carella knew there was no time to raise the pistol. He knew there was no time to scramble away, no time to dodge the blow, the axe was already at its apogee, it would descend in another split instant.

Whitson threw himself for what seemed the length of the basement, sailing into the air in a flying leap, the entire huge and muscular hulk of him colliding with Iverson's immense body. Iverson staggered back against the furnace and the axe head crashed against the cast iron door with a furiously ringing clang, and then fell clattering to the cement floor. Iverson pushed himself off the furnace and reached for the axe again, but Whitson had drawn back his right hand, the fist bunched, and then his arm shot out with stunning force, straight and true and unerring, and Iverson's head snapped back as though his neck were broken, and he collapsed to the floor.

'You okay?' Hawes asked.

'I'm okay,' Carella said. 'Sam?'

'I'm fine,' Whitson said.

'He did it for the wood business,' Hawes said, astonished. 'He did it for the lousy two-bit wood business.'

I did it for the wood business, Iverson said.

I did it because he stole the wood business from me. The wood business was my idea. Before I became super in 4113, the fireplaces was all boarded up and plastered up. It was me who made the fireplaces work, gave the tenants heat. It was me who first thought up the idea of the wood business.

George stole the business from me.

First he starts bringing in big logs from the country where he lives, him and his crazy wife. Then he steals the handyman away from me, he offers him fifty cents an hour to chop up the logs, sure he's going to take it, who wouldn't? I don't mind when he sells the wood to his own tenants, that's his building, he can do what he wants. But then he starts selling to my tenants, and that I don't like.

When I go down the basement next door the beginning of the year to tell him about it, I didn't mean to kill him. He's sitting there counting his money, putting it in a coffee can, writing down his sales in a black book, putting that in the coffee can, too. When I tell him he has to leave my tenants alone, he starts to laugh. So I went out back to the toolshed and then I came down the basement again with the axe. When he sees the axe, he starts laughing again, so I hit him. He comes at me, and he grabs for my clothes, but I keep hitting him, and finally I hit him across the throat, I know he is dead from that one but I keep hitting him anyway, and he falls down, and I put the axe in his head and ,leave it there.

I emptied the money from the coffee can, there was seven dollars and fifty cents, it rightfully belonged to me. I also took the black book because half the tenants in it, they belong to me . . .

I wiped off the shelf and also the coffee can. I didn't want to leave no fingerprints. Then I filled the coffee can with things from the other cans, so no one would know there'd been money in it.

I killed that policeman, too.

I went down there to look for my button. George ripped one of the buttons from my overalls when we were fighting down there, and I knew if somebody found the button, I would be in trouble. So I kept going down to look for it, and the day I found it, there was that cop down there, too. He saw the button, so I had to kill him. That was all there was to it. I would have killed the handyman today, too, but he was too strong for me.

I never killed anybody before George in my life.

He shouldn't have stolen the wood business from me.

On his way home that night, Steve Carella stopped into the bookstore called The Bookends in Riverhead. It was close to seven o'clock, and they were getting ready to close the shop, but he found Allie the Shark Spedino sitting behind his cash register and watching the few remaining customers in the store.

'Uh-oh,' Spedino said. 'Trouble.'

'No trouble,' Carella answered.

'Then what brings the Law here?' Spedino asked.

'Three things.'

'Like?'

'Like one, we found the killer. You can stop worrying.'

'Who was worrying?' Spedino said. 'I don't know what *you* thought, but I knew I didn't do it.'

'Number two, no more crap games in our precinct, Spedino.'

'What crap games? I haven't been to a crap game in . . .'

'Spedino, don't snow me. We know you were there. I'm telling you no more crap games or I go straight to your wife. Okay?'

'Okay, okay.' Spedino shook his head. 'Boy.'

'And number three, I'd like to buy a rhyming dictionary.'

'A what?'

'A rhyming dictionary,' Carella said.

'What for?'

'I promised somebody I'd find a rhyme.'

'Okay,' Spedino said, and he shook his head again. 'Boy.'

Carella left the shop with the dictionary under his arm. Night had come upon the city suddenly, and the streets were dark and bitter cold. He walked to where he had parked his car, and then he sniffed deeply of the brittle air and opened the car door and slid onto the seat.

For a moment, he sat looking through the windshield at the city, locked in upon itself, the barren January streets, the flickering neon, the black sky behind the silent buildings. For a moment

. . . only for a moment . . . the city overwhelmed him and he sat in almost stunned silence and thought of the poor goddamn janitor in a slum building who'd killed another man for what amounted to a few dollars a week.

He hunched his shoulders against the cold. He started the engine and turned on the heater, and slowly edged the car out into the traffic.

Books should be returned on or before the
last date stamped below.

NORTH EAST of SCOTLAND LIBRARY SERVICE
MELDRUM MEG WAY, OLDMELDRUM